ABOUT THE
DARK HART COLLECTION

THE DARK HART COLLECTION is a line of novels and novellas curated by me, Sadie Hartmann, aka "Mother Horror," for Dark Matter INK. These stories map new territories in the ever-evolving landscape of the horror genre. I invite you to escape into books written by authors who blur the lines between multiple genres, and who explore the depth and breadth of dark hearts everywhere.

Sincerely,

Sadie Hartmann
Curator, The Dark Hart Collection

Books in the Conjure Series

ROOTWORK

A GATHERING OF WEAPONS

Other Books in the Dark Hart Collection

MOSAIC by Catherine McCarthy

APPARITIONS by Adam Pottle

I CAN SEE YOUR LIES by Izzy Lee

PRAISE FOR
THE CONJURE SERIES

"*A Gathering of Weapons* is a worthy follow-up to *Rootwork* in that it brings the character of Pee Wee back to the forefront with such visceral passion. Tracy Cross deftly weaves enchanting stories that tell about the character's growth, both physically and spiritually, as she learns more and more of what it means to be a conjure woman. This book brims with cultural significance and beautiful storytelling. When you read this, you won't be disappointed."

—Scott A. Johnson, author of *Through the Witches Stone, Ungeheuer,* and *Shy Grove: A Ghost Story*

"*Rootwork* is one part magical realism, one part coming of age story, one part examination of American identity, and all parts pure magic. It's unique and spellbinding, and I loved it."

—Lisa Morton, six-time winner of the Bram Stoker Award

"*Rootwork* fearlessly brings folk horror to the Deep South. Tracy Cross paints a dark portrait of Black family life, with all the wisdom of our ancestors—their accomplishments, their sorrows, their unresolved hope and rage—and in doing so delivers uniquely American horror without pulling any punches. If you're a fan of historical fiction and tales of the supernatural, this book will resonate with you long after you're done reading it."

—John Edward Lawson, author of *Bibliophobia*

"With *Rootwork*, Tracy Cross introduces herself to readers as a gifted storyteller of the highest order. This is a richly folkloric tale of traditions passed down, of community and family, and the lasting links forged through the shared experiences of sisters and the impenetrable bonds that anchor them to their histories and each other. At the heart of *Rootwork* is its plucky, free-spirited heroine, Pee Wee Conway, who is certain to beguile readers of all ages."

—Vince A. Liaguno, Bram Stoker Award-winning editor of *Unspeakable Horror: From the Shadows of the Closet* and *Other Tales: An Inclusive Anthology*

"Rootwork transported me to another world, on I was unfamiliar with but thoroughly enjoyed. Blending history, Hoodoo, and horror elements, Tracy Cross delivers a compelling narrative with characters I sincerely hope to meet again. I really did feel like I was right there alongside Pee Wee and Aunt Teddy."

—Janine Pipe, Splatterpunk Award-nominated author of *Sausages: The Making of Dog Soldiers*

"The power and promise of fiction is the ability to take you places you can't go and do things you'll never do with people you'll never meet. Rootwork delivers on that promise with an engrossing coming-of-age tale set amid the Voodoo and Hoodoo of backcountry Louisiana in 1889. Tracy Cross works magic with the characters and setting of her debut novel. You will love this book and the people in it."

—F. Paul Wilson, author of *The Keep*

THE CONJURE SERIES

A GATHERING OF WEAPONS

Edited by Rob Carroll
Book Design and Layout by Rob Carroll
Cover Design by Rob Carroll
Author photo by Mig Dooley

ISBN 978-1-958598-38-2 (paperback)
ISBN 978-1-958598-84-9 (eBook)

darkmatter-ink.com

THE CONJURE SERIES

A GATHERING OF WEAPONS

TRACY CROSS

To R for helping me to overcome my past and move into the future.

WHAT IS HOODOO?

THE CONJURE SERIES by Tracy Cross is a tale of historical fiction and folk horror inspired by the culture and traditions of Hoodoo and the author's familial history in the American South. Not to be confused with Voodoo (also explored in the series), Hoodoo is a set of spiritual practices, traditions, and beliefs that were created by enslaved African Americans in the Southern United States. Also known as rootwork or *conjure*, practitioners of Hoodoo were known as rootworkers, conjure doctors, or conjure men and conjure women. The events in this book are mostly fiction, but the cultural and spiritual history upon which they are based is real.

FROM THE AUTHOR:

Black cat bone. Goofer dust. Sinner man hand. These are all aspects of Hoodoo, but what is it?

Hoodoo combines African spirituality and religious doctrine to create magic that can conjure a curse against an enemy, or remove a curse from a friend. In this book,

Hoodoo is practiced by Christian folks who will even pray to the Holy Trinity as part of their invocations. Generally speaking, Hoodoo was a way for Black folks to explain bad luck, because, for example, someone had planted a "root" on you. But mostly, Hoodoo was a way to fix things or make things right in the world. Putting roots on an abusive slave owner and their family was one way for a Hoodoo practitioner to enact justice.

Some might think that the practice and its effects have died out, but this is not true. Hoodoo is eternal.

LOUISIANA

1893

THE WEAPONS

A PARTIAL LIST of the many weapons Pee Wee keeps in her conjure bag or near her person at all times:

1. Black cat bone from Pa
2. Handkerchief from Ma
3. Black button from Ann
4. White button from Ann
5. Pennies from a preacher man's grave
6. Trinkets from Aunt Teddy
7. Chicken bones from her village/one of Betty's stews
8. Shiny beads from Viola
9. Shiny marbles from Viola
10. A shell from Lone Wolf
11. A shiny piece of glass from her home
12. A small collection of seashells she found over time
13. Jawbone from a hanged man
14. Rib from an unborn child (she made Bump get that for her)

15. Small bottle of rum she stole from Aunt Teddy

16. Graveyard nails from a coffin

17. Cigar stub she found at Viola's house

18. Dried herbs from the sundown town

19. Hot foot powder

20. Teeth, bones, feathers, and amulets from the graveyard

21. Small piece of an iron rod to drive into the ground during a thunderstorm

22. Dried chicken feet

23. Red-and-black fabric to make small gris gris bags

24. Fresh mint for asthma

25. Marbles she stole from Bump

26. Cinnamon sticks she keeps bundled in a red bow

27. A pair of dice she stole from Bump's game

28. Lots of sage to protect herself from evil

29. Basil to protect from evil entities

30. A silver fork to keep witches from riding her body

31. Small bottles with love potions she's started

32. Love powder (her own creation)

33. A dead man's hand

34. A finger from a different dead man's hand

35. Shoestrings

36. A change of underwear

VIOLA AND THE SINNER-MAN HAND

"AUNT TEDDY IS gonna kill me!"

As Pee Wee half-ran, half-skipped down the street outside the bakery, she stripped off the ankle-length skirt she wore over the dark-colored pants cuffed above her ankle boots. The pants made her look taller, but her nickname wasn't Pee Wee because she was the youngest of her sisters. She was tiny, with a headful of tightly coiled black curls and skin the color of pecans. She stuffed the skirt into the black handmade conjure bag with her Hoodoo potions and money.

She chided herself for getting home late again. "Shouldn't have been runnin' my mouth with chef. But those pralines were really good. Especially the extra ones he added for free." She patted the bag and the soft pralines wrapped in several layers of white paper.

While running, she fixed some hair pins to her hair and tied the curls down with a black headscarf. Her hair needed to stay clean for another week.

The sun dipped below the horizon as she walked down the worn path in the woods toward Aunt Teddy's house.

She'd been living with Aunt Teddy since the flood in the summer of 1889. Now at age thirteen, Pee Wee was a practicing conjure girl. She didn't like the term, but loved to practice. Aunt Teddy called her a conjure girl, but if Pee Wee could get a job, she'd be a "full-fledged practicin' conjure *woman*."

Aunt Teddy's first house was near a river. But after the flood a few years ago, Teddy found an even taller stilt house that seemed to reach as high as the surrounding trees. Pee Wee didn't like this new house as much as the old one—where she and her two sisters had lived with Aunt Teddy that fateful summer—but it would have to do. She often wondered if the ghosts of her and her sisters practicing Hoodoo still inhabited that land where that old place once stood.

This new house was farther inland, away from the water and close to the cemetery where Teddy wanted to be buried, a fact she never let Pee Wee forget.

"Are you listenin' to me, Hattie Mae?" she'd said. *"That's where I want to be buried! Nowhere else!"*

Pee Wee was working hard, kneading bread dough in a huge yellow bowl.

"Aunt Teddy, you ain't got to say it but once. I know! And y'know I prefer 'Pee Wee' on account of Hattie Mae being my business name."

"I calls you Hattie Mae when I'm serious about somethin'. Besides, if'n I call you Pee Wee, you ain't gonna listen none."

Aunt Teddy walked over and took the bowl from her niece. The bread dough had been kneaded and punched down so many times in anger that Pee Wee was sure the loaf was ruined.

Pee Wee continued down the forest path. Beneath the scent of rotten trees and wildflowers was a heavier smell of earthiness and a feeling of dampness in the air. A static in the atmosphere hinted that something big was about to happen.

Pee Wee stopped and looked around. The sky was a dark, reddish hue, and the sunset was now casting long shadows across the forest floor. She imagined hearing birds calling to their young, telling the fledglings to return home, knowing she should follow suit. Frogs croaked nearby as she wiped at the perspiration that was building up on her brow. Beads of salty sweat shimmied down between her shoulder blades as she pressed forward. The more she moved, the more her shirt and cuffed pants felt sticky from the humidity.

In the distance, something beckoned her. It danced around in the air—yellowish and red, with a mind of its own. Heavy smoke rose and swirled around it. Soon, the smoke was on top of her, filling her lungs and making her cough. She pulled her shirt up to cover her mouth as she stumbled backward off the path. This was no ordinary fire. Pee Wee could feel the heat from quite a distance away.

She retrieved a purple pouch and a small bottle of rum from the black conjure bag at her hip. She poured some powder from the pouch into her hand, took a sip of the rum, then held out her hand and opened it, palm to the sky, to present the small mound of powder to her lips. She blew the powder to the wind.

"Open my eyes and show me the truth," she said.

She closed her eyes and blew at the powder again.

"Open my eyes and show me the truth!" she said, more demanding this time. She steadied her feet on the ground.

She was shown a blazing fire. Voices whispered on the winds around her.

Pee Wee pressed a hand to a blackened tree trunk and closed her eyes. She asked the tree to tell her what happened. She took slow, easy breaths, just like Aunt Teddy's boyfriend Lone Wolf taught her. Her fingernails scraped at the black bark.

"Open to me and tell me your story."

The longer her hand lingered on the tree, the more she felt compelled to look up toward the spindly dead branches, where something was wrapped in rope and smoking.

It was a body.

Stumbling backward, Pee Wee fell to the ground. She apologized to the tree, then pulled a dagger from her boot, climbed to her feet, and pushed her way through the bushes behind her. As she felt her way through the dark, something small and warm trembled at her feet.

Her heart pounded and her body tensed as she slowly turned to see what it was. But before she could, a hand covered her mouth, silencing the scream that tried to escape.

"They gonna getcha too, if'n ya don't stay quiet!"

Pee Wee was pulled into a small bush with the person and discovered them to be a girl about the age of ten. Pee Wee stared into the girl's dark eyes. Her skin was soft and covered with dirt, and her hand had an earthy smell.

"What the…?" Pee Wee whispered once the hand was removed.

"I gotta get away," the girl whispered. "They done killed my family. I ain't got nowhere to go, and they gon' kill me too."

"Who is you?"

"Name's Viola. My mama was married to a rich white man, and the white men in the town wanted our land. I guess they was sick of fightin' for it, cuz they came and burned my whole house down tonight. That's mama hangin' up there. They dipped her in somethin' like oil and burned her, then strung her up in that tree."

Something fell to the ground behind them, and Pee Wee jumped. Viola's hand shot out and covered Pee Wee's mouth again.

Pee Wee tried to see what had hit the ground with such a terrible thud, but Viola stopped her, seemed to read her mind and wanted to spare her the trauma. "That sound ya heard, it's all that's left of my baby brother. Mama was pregnant. It's best ya not look at his remains."

Pee Wee's mouth fell open. She imagined the baby still attached to its mama via the umbilical cord, and she grew dizzy and nauseous from the thought. "H-how you know it's a boy? How y'know it's your brother?"

"Mama had the sight. She knew it before she was even pregnant."

A small whimper escaped Pee Wee's lips. "Don't make no sense. Ain't nobody been hung round here by no white men for some time." *How could men do that to a pregnant woman?* she thought. *The devil got them good.*

Viola grabbed Pee Wee's wrist. "No time for debatin'. We gotta go over yonder." Viola crawled out of the bush, leaving Pee Wee sitting on her behind.

Pee Wee glanced back at the small lump that had fallen from its mama's belly before crawling after Viola in tears.

"Viola, stop. We far enough. We can talk now."

"Whatchu wanna talk 'bout, Pee Wee?"

Pee Wee sat back on her heels and stared. "How y'know my name?"

The moonlight shining through the branches made Viola's honey-colored skin look speckled with dots. She laughed but didn't answer Pee Wee's question.

Pee Wee leaned against a fallen tree and swatted at a bunch of gnats hovering near her face. "How old is you?"

"I guess I'm about twelve. I don't know."

"How ya don't know how old you is? Everybody know they age," Pee Wee said, studying Viola with a skeptical eye. Viola's hair was a mess of untamed black curls, and she had red scratches from the bushes on her face and hands. She wore a plain black dress and her feet were dirty.

Unnerved by how Pee Wee was looking at her, Viola covered the marks on her hands and pulled her legs beneath the dress. She snapped a twig off a nearby bush and twisted it in her fingers. "One of them men was gonna take me away and make me have some babies with him, but I ain't want that."

She paused, then added, "I want to be free."

Pee Wee shuddered. She'd never heard someone speak like this before. She remembered what Aunt Teddy had told her about slaves, but that wasn't happening now or ever again, at least according to her aunt. But Pee Wee knew these woods were a strange place, and she had seen many strange things here before.

"*When* is you from?"

"Do it matter?"

"Yeah, it do. When you from?" Pee Wee stood and wiped the dirt from her pants. "Ya ain't got no shoes, and I ain't seen clothes like that round here before. When you from? You some kinda ghost or somethin'?"

Viola stood and faced Pee Wee. "So what if I was? Whatchu gonna do 'bout it?"

Pee Wee put her hands on her hips and cocked one hip to the side. "I can break the spell and send ya home. That's what. I'm a conjure woman, y'know."

"I know whatchu are, Pee Wee. These woods are filled with ghosts, and they all talk about you. As a matter of fact, I been searchin' for ya. I need yo' help, see. But we need to hurry, cuz them men gonna come back and get me, and I don't want that. Last time, they called me a witch and burned me alive."

"Watchu mean 'the last time'? You ain't makin' no sense, Viola."

"Time ain't the same for a ghost, Pee Wee."

Pee Wee crossed her arms on her chest. "Well, is you? Is you a witch, Viola?"

Viola stared at Pee Wee with eyes black as flint. Looking at them was like staring into the darkness.

Pee Wee thought about digging into her conjure bag and pulling out her mojo pack that Aunt Teddy had made for her. Thought about using it to send Viola on her ghostly way, but she decided against it. She wasn't afraid of Viola, she was intrigued by her. Maybe Viola could even teach her a thing or two about witchcraft.

"Somethin' like that," said Viola. "Now come with me 'fore it's too late. I gotta give ya somethin', but I don't have it with me. We have to go get it." Viola extended her hand out to Pee Wee. "Please."

"I'll hold my own hand, thank you."

Pee Wee and Viola ran through the woods until Pee Wee felt something familiar about the location. She'd walked this path before. She knew this area, knew the marks on the trees that showed how high the waters were back when the town flooded. She recognized the faint smell of stew boiling with fresh herbs and vegetables from the garden, even found the spiderwebs to be familiar. This was where she had lived with her ma and pa and sisters before her pa was killed and the flood washed everything away.

Everything was abandoned now. All the houses looked sad and falling apart, and the world was blanketed in fog. The houses shimmered in and out of history.

Pee Wee stopped in her tracks. Down a path where the air was clear and small stones shone in the moonlight, a haint-blue house stood alone. The woods were dense around the house as if the trees had crowded together to keep it hidden from anyone who might come looking for it. The haint-blue exterior was covered with strange black markings.

The sounds of frogs croaking and birds chirping faded away. And when Pee Wee stepped on a twig and it snapped, it made no sound.

"Where are we?" she asked.

"It's a place I call Nowhere. It's between your time and mine. Sometimes, I can make it through, and sometimes I can't. I hate this place because I can't leave without help. You the only one that can do it, Pee Wee. The only one that can get me outta here." Viola walked to the house and went inside. Moments later, she came back out with something wrapped in a black cloth. She handed it to Pee Wee and told her to take it.

Pee Wee took the thing in the black cloth and unwrapped it, nearly gasping at the sight. Inside the wrapping was a shriveled hand, a thumb and two fingers outstretched.

"It's a sinner-man hand. I need you to—"

Pee Wee tossed the hand to the ground and stepped back. It had looked and smelled fresh, like someone had just cut it from a body. She thought she had seen the fingers move a bit, and she wondered if the hand would now get up on its own and crawl away. The odor of rot and blood filled her nostrils, causing her to release what was still undigested in her stomach.

"You just cost me my pralines," Pee Wee whimpered. She wiped her mouth as the sour smell of sick filled the air between them.

"I need ya to wish on the hand. Wish me away, Pee Wee."

"I don't understand. Why can't you do it?"

"And here I was thinkin' you wanted to learn somethin'. Some conjure woman you are."

Pee Wee wanted to learn, but she also knew that Aunt Teddy would never teach her about wishing on a sinner-man hand. This was dark magic, something the devil himself tossed at her feet.

Viola picked up the hand, and the three outstretched digits curled inward to make a fist. "I used my wishes already, see. No more fingers. I need you to do this for me. Please."

Pee Wee tapped a finger on her chin and thought. Could Viola be the woman that used to lurk around this village when Pee Wee was younger? The one that appeared the night of her father's funeral and beckoned for Pee Wee to come to her burned shell of a house?

Was Viola the Voodoo lady?

As if reading Pee Wee's mind, Viola spoke: "They was just scared of what they didn't know. In reality, I ain't no different than your Aunt Teddy. I've been tryin' to call you, tryin' to reach out to you since you was just a child. I wanted to teach you Voodoo so you could save your daddy. I saw what them men did to him, and I didn't like it. But no matter what I tried, you would never come to me." Viola sighed. "I tried walkin' in your dreams. Even tried leavin' trinkets by your house, but your mama swept them all away. I only ever wanted to help."

"Maybe so. But that still don't answer my question. Why you need me?"

Viola sighed. "I'm allowed to come back to this world one night a year, on the night them men killed my family, which is tonight, but I got stuck here this time, and I can't get back to the spirit realm. That's why I need you to wish me away."

Pee Wee crossed her arms. "But if'n I did that, you couldn't teach me whatchu know."

"Listen, you is touched, which means you can do this without me. You can teach yourself. You just need the proper learnin' tools. And everythin' I know is inside that house."

"Aunt Teddy say touched people is crazy."

"You seem right as rain to me, and we here standin' face to face. Do *you* think you're crazy, Pee Wee?"

Pee Wee shook her head no. A million questions swirled inside her head.

"You ready now? Cuz we gotta hurry."

Pee Wee walked up to the house and touched the door, felt some kind of magic run through her. It was the feeling of spells being cast and chants being performed. It was the vision of charms being summoned and people being helped.

But there was also the vision of people being harmed—

Viola pointed to the woods. "They comin'!"

Pee Wee looked back to see the faint glimmer of blazing torches moving through the trees. The scent of burning bushes and the odor of death and decay had led them toward the house.

Viola tossed the hand to Pee Wee, and Pee Wee watched as the two fingers and the thumb stretched themselves out again. She looked at Viola. "So I get three wishes with this. Then what?"

"Then you need to give it to someone else."

"Why should I waste a wish on you? What stops me from runnin' away and leavin' ya here to die, over and over again, from now until eternity?"

"Cuz you got a good heart, Pee Wee. Everybody say so. And I promise to teach you what I can through the house."

"How long I have the wishes for?"

"Until you use 'em all up. Now, please!"

"You best stop rushin' me," Pee Wee snapped, "else I'll wish ya here forever!" She looked back at the men with torches. Their faces were strange—white and oblong, with dark holes for their eyes and mouths. Their feet didn't quite touch the ground, but they didn't quite float, either. She could smell the scent of burning torches now.

Raising the sinner man hand towards the men, Pee Wee made her first wish and wished them away forever—to Hell, where they belonged. The middle finger on the hand curled closed. One by one, the men disappeared in shrieks of agony.

Pee Wee then turned to Viola and held the hand toward her. "If'n you been lyin', Viola, you will stay here forever and never leave this parish. But if ya been tellin' the truth, I wish you into the afterlife with yo' family."

The index finger on the hand curled closed, and when Pee Wee looked up, Viola was gone.

She had one wish left.

Pee Wee placed a hand on the house and felt even more of its energy surge within her. It was a greedy type of energy, the kind that gave you more power the longer you touched it. She saw things she wouldn't understand for a long time.

Someone touched her back, and the vision disappeared. She whipped around to see Aunt Teddy, lantern in hand, glaring down at her.

"Aunt Teddy! Whatchu doin' here?"

Pee Wee quickly hid the sinner-man hand behind her back, where she stuffed it into the waistline of her pants.

"Lone Wolf saw you stumblin' this way, and I came to see if you was okay." Aunt Teddy lowered the lantern so that it was near to the ground. She pointed at the pile of sick. "Looks like you been sneakin' off and eatin' pralines again."

Pee Wee shrugged.

Aunt Teddy looked up the house, a stern look in her eyes. "What brought you here, Pee Wee?" she asked.

Pee Wee shrugged again.

"This place ain't no good for you," Aunt Teddy said. "This here was a bad place. Home to a crazy lady named Viola. She was a Voodoo woman, and she did some terrible things in her time. Now c'mon. We goin' home."

Aunt Teddy started up the path, but Pee Wee turned back to the house and placed her hand on the door once more. Something warm filled her body. The walls glowed red as she looked around at all the magic she couldn't see before. With Viola's help, Pee Wee would become the most powerful conjure woman ever. She could feel it.

When Aunt Teddy looked back, she couldn't see the glow of the house. She just saw Pee Wee refusing to come along "Come now, child! It's time to go!"

Pee Wee blinked. She could now see that Aunt Teddy had a blue aura about her. She blinked several more times before grabbing her conjure bag and discreetly sticking the sinner-man hand inside.

"Whatchu just put in yo' bag?" Aunt Teddy asked.

"Uh… More pralines."

Aunt Teddy tsked and continued on her way. "You gonna make yourself sick again," she said over her shoulder.

One more wish.

"I'll be fine," Pee Wee said.

JUNIOR AND THE DOLL

"I DON'T UNDERSTAND why we need to wear these clothes. All we doin' is sellin' stuff by the road."

Pee Wee struggled with the basket of Aunt Teddy's handmade conjure bags.

Lone Wolf set his heavy bags down near the roadside stand. "I told you. We must look presentable. Who do you think people are more likely to buy a conjure bag from? A proper salesman, or an Indian?"

"Prob'ly a Injun," Pee Wee replied. She grunted as she set the basket on the ground.

"Grammar," Lone Wolf said, touching Pee Wee on the tip of her nose with his finger. "Try again."

"Prob'ly *an* Injun. Better?" Pee Wee hated how Lone Wolf and her Aunt Teddy were such sticklers for language. All she needed to know was how to do root-work. She was thirteen now, time for her to go out and make a living.

Lone Wolf stood taller than the average man and was twice as graceful as any woman. He took off his black fedora and suit jacket, then rolled up his sleeves and started setting out their wares. Pee Wee—knee-high to a grasshopper—helped him, and soon they had a stand full of fruit, vegetables, and small red conjure bags to sell to passing travelers.

"Think we gonna sell a lot today?" Pee Wee asked, stepping back into the shade to sit on a log beneath a tree.

"Depends." Lone Wolf's voice was deep and seemed to rumble around Pee Wee's insides when he spoke. His brown skin shone in the sunlight as he readjusted his clothing and stood straight.

"Depends on what?"

"Just depends," Lone Wolf replied.

Pee Wee fidgeted with the black dress that hung off her slender frame like laundry. Her black hair was pulled into a tight ponytail, and she wore a white straw hat.

"Do you work with Bump at the butcher shop today?" Lone Wolf asked.

"Yeah," said Pee Wee. She stopped and corrected herself: "I mean, *yes.*"

Lone Wolf smiled and nodded. "What time do you have to work?"

"After we finish here, which if'n ya ask me, won't take long as I don't see us sellin' a bunch in this location. I still think we shoulda went to the settlement. They woulda bought us outta conjure bags and then some."

After an hour at the roadside, half their inventory remained. Pee Wee leaned forward and watched a solitary figure skip down the road toward them. She shielded her eyes from the bright sun to see the person clearer: a young girl no bigger than Pee Wee, who looked also to be about the same age.

The girl stopped in front of the stand. She had wild, copper-colored hair, tanned skin, and freckles all over her face. When she smiled, she looked like she was up to something. She wore a green dress that hung off one shoulder, white socks, and black ankle boots.

"Can I help you?" Pee Wee asked. The girl was actually a bit shorter than her, and Pee Wee was thrilled to be looking down at someone for a change.

The girl giggled. She ignored Pee Wee and addressed Lone Wolf instead. "My mama wants some of them conjure bags. How much for three of 'em?" The girl crossed her arms over her chest and jutted her left hip out farther than was normal.

"Three for a dollar. Unless you have something to trade," Lone Wolf said.

The girl glanced at Pee Wee and leaned over to pull a dollar bill from her sock. "That's kinda high, mister."

Pee Wee blocked Lone Wolf's hand with her own, "Then you can make yo' own. Now git on!" Pee Wee shooed at the girl.

"Fine," the girl huffed. "I guess I'll take 'em." She unfolded the bill and handed it to Pee Wee. Lone Wolf told the girl about each bag so that she could make an informed choice, but the girl only half-listened and kept glancing at Pee Wee.

"Whatchu want?" Pee Wee finally snapped.

"Pee Wee!" Lone Wolf scolded.

"What? She keep lookin' at me like she know me. You don't know me, girl." Pee Wee crossed her arms over her chest and jutted her hip out even farther than the girl had.

The girl tilted her head to the side and smiled at Pee Wee. "Yes, I do, Pee Wee Conway. And you know me, too. I'm Junior. We went to school together. I was in yo' class. "

"You don't look like no junior. You's a girl."

The tension between the two girls was enough to make Lone Wolf step in between them, like he was breaking up a fight between two growling hound dogs.

"Creole Kate is my mama. That's my name, too. Only I's Creole Kate Junior, so everybody just call me Junior, on count."

Pee Wee closed the small distance between them and eyed the girl. "I don't remember you from school."

"I sat in the back of class. When I came. Most days, my mama taught me at home in the swamp, until she pulled me from school. Said I was wastin' my time there."

"Sounds like she shoulda kept you enrolled cuz you cain't talk worth a damn. Not proper, anyways."

Lone Wolf cleared his throat and separated the girls again.

Pee Wee wondered about the girl's race. "What are you? I's curious." She glanced at Lone Wolf, "I mean, *I'm* curious."

"I'm mixed. My mama is white, but my daddy was a Black man, big and tall. Thick like a tree."

"*Was?*"

"That sheriff shot him down. Accused my daddy of gamblin' or runnin' numbers or somethin'. Now it's just me and my mama. We live in the woods over yonder. So, 'bout these conjure bags ya sellin'—"

"Whatcha wanna know?" Pee Wee put her hand on her hip to match Junior.

"It ain't what I wanna know, it's whatchu *need* to know."

Pee Wee laughed and glanced at Lone Wolf. "What can you teach me that I don't already know?"

"Lotsa stuff."

Lone Wolf checked the time on his pocket watch. "You can head on over to the butcher shop now, Pee Wee. I think we're done for the day," he said, hoping this would put an end to the conversation.

But it didn't end it. Only put it on pause.

Pee Wee pointed at Junior. "You wait here. I gotta change clothes quick, but you and I ain't finished."

Junior nodded, and Pee Wee grabbed a sack off the ground and slipped into the trees to undress. When she stepped back out, she was wearing a pair of black overalls and ragged ankle boots that Lone Wolf had repaired a million times over. Beneath the overalls, she wore a white T-shirt. Her hair was still snatched back into a tight ponytail at the nape of her neck.

"Why you have to change for the butcher shop?" Junior asked.

"It's my other job, and I don't go time to waste, so we's gonna have to walk and talk." She started down the road and Junior followed her. "Lone Wolf," Pee Wee said over her shoulder, "can you take my stuff home please?"

Lone Wolf nodded and sat down on the shady log to rest. He waved goodbye to Pee Wee and Junior, then pulled out a pipe and lit it.

"Why you work at a butcher shop?" Junior asked after they'd walked a bit alongside the road.

"Cuz my cousin Bump is a butcher. I help him out, killin' chickens and such."

"Do you wanna be a butcher?" Junior asked.

"No, I'm a conjure woman."

Junior laughed too hard for her own good.

Pee Wee clenched her teeth and made a fist with her right hand. She really wanted to slug Junior into the road, where hopefully she'd get hit by a wagon or trolley or somethin'. But instead, she dug her fingernails into her palm and kept walking. She motioned for them to cross the street.

Dogs roamed the sidewalks while musicians played on the corners for a little extra change in their hats. A few musicians who knew Pee Wee nodded in her direction when she danced past. Her nostrils filled with the smells of fresh-baked bread, pies, and her favorite sweets: caramels.

They strolled by the town brothel, and a few of the women leaned out the window and tossed Pee Wee a few coins and requests for love bags. Pee Wee stopped and pulled a tablet and a pencil from the front pocket of her overalls. She wrote each order down and picked up the coins from the sidewalk with Junior's help.

Junior tried to read what Pee Wee wrote. "I can help you make those bags."

"Did I ask for your help? I think not." Pee Wee skipped ahead. "Now hurry. I don't wanna be late."

Pee Wee and Junior arrived at the butcher shop and ran around back. Bump stood outside, waiting with an apron and a cleaver for Pee Wee.

Junior stared wide-eyed at Bump. He was an impressive sight. When he was younger, he was smaller than Pee Wee, but now he was twice her height and three times her size, with broad shoulders, big arms, and a powerful chest. He crossed his muscled arms over themselves and grinned at Pee Wee. His chestnut-colored skin glistened with sweat.

"I need ten chickens today. You up to it?" Bump's voice had grown deeper as he matured and was now like one of them big instruments the men on the corner played— what was it called again? A bass? Either way, every word sounded like it had been dipped in the sweetest butter and seasoned with a pinch of southern twang.

"Yeah, Bump. Help me get this apron on." Pee Wee turned so her back was to him. She raised her arms, and he tied the apron snuggly around her waist.

Bump looked to Junior. "Who's your friend?"

"Her name is Junior. Her mama is Creole Kate. Y'know her?" Pee Wee took the cleaver.

"Can't say I do."

A bell rang, and Bump ran back inside the shop to greet the customer. He stopped in the doorway and turned to Pee Wee. "Ten fully dressed chickens. Got it?"

"Yeah. Er, I mean, *yes*."

"And get rid of Junior. If'n Mr. Frank see her, we both gonna have some problems."

Once Bump was out of sight, Junior turned to Pee Wee. "You say that's your cousin?" she asked.

Pee Wee rolled her eyes. The lust in Junior's voice was obvious. "We grew up together. He like a brother to me."

Junior fanned herself. "How's the pay in a place like this?"

"It's enough for me to do what I gotta."

Junior smiled. "*Enough?* When it comes to money, there ain't never *enough*. What if I taught you how to make lots of money? Lots more than you make here."

Pee Wee wrestled a chicken from the cage and snapped its neck before laying it across a block and chopping its head off. "I'm listenin'."

Junior lowered her voice to a whisper. "The real money is in sellin' white folks Voodoo."

Pee Wee stopped and stared at Junior. She thought of Viola. "I dunno. My aunt told me not to mess with that stuff. Dark magic and all."

Junior pointed at the ground in front of Pee Wee. "You already choppin' the heads off chickens. You basically doin' Voodoo already."

Pee Wee continued with her work. "I gotta think about it."

"Voodoo ain't all bad. It's Catholic, y'know."

Pee Wee mumbled, "All that standin' and sittin' and beads. They got like fifty thousand prayers for—"

"Not all Catholics are like that," said Junior. "We brought stuff from Africa into it."

Pee Wee stopped and looked at this mixed girl telling her about Africa. "Get outta here, Junior. I got work to do."

Junior smiled at Pee Wee and took a step toward her. She looked her dead in the eyes as she reached up and quickly plucked a few strands of Pee Wee's hair from her head.

Pee Wee's hands were full, or else she would have decked her.

"What is you doin'?" Pee Wee yelled. "You can't just walk up to a person and—"

Bump stuck his head out the back door and used his thumb to make a slicing motion across his neck. He then pointed at Junior. "You! Get outta here!"

Junior cackled as she skipped off down the street.

AFTER WORK, PEE Wee told Bump all about her run-in with Junior on their walk back to Aunt Teddy's house.

"And then she pulled some of my hair out my head!" she said.

"Why ya s'pose she did that?" Bump asked, biting down on a biscuit he'd taken on the way out of the butcher shop.

"I dunno. But she lucky my hands were tied up."

Pee Wee felt a sharp pain in her stomach and stopped walking.

"What's wrong?"

"I dunno. Feels strange. Maybe it's somethin' I ate." She doubled over and snapped her knees together. A wave of nausea swept over her as she dropped to the ground. She put her hands on the sidewalk and loosed everything in her stomach.

"Sweet Jesus, Pee Wee!" Bump exclaimed.

Pee Wee looked up from her sick and quickly surveyed her surroundings. The people around her had all stopped to stare. It felt like a thousand eyes were on her. Music stopped playing, and a little boy ran over with a jar of water. Something felt wrong inside Pee Wee, and that's when she saw Junior across the street with a doll in her hand, smiling.

"That's why she took my hair! And why my stomach hurts! Bump, it's Junior! Get her!"

But by the time Bump looked to where Pee Wee was pointing, Junior was already gone. And when he looked back, Pee Wee fainted.

PEE WEE WOKE to Aunt Teddy, Lone Wolf, Cousin Skeet, and Bump talking in the living room of Aunt Teddy's house. The sweet smells of magnolia and jasmine swirled in the air. Depending on where a person stood, the house would also smell of peppermint. Maybe a hint of cinnamon in the dining room. Breezes of lavender swirled from the bedroom on the summer breeze. The floor of the house was wood and seemed to groan as people walked across it. Aunt Teddy often promised to fix the groaning, but never did.

"What'd ya see?" Teddy asked Bump.

"Not much. We was just walkin', and then she got sick on the sidewalk. Said somethin' 'bout this girl she was with earlier—name was Junior—told me to get her, but when I looked at where Pee Wee was pointin', there was no one there."

Cousin Skeet jumped in. "Lemme rattle this boy's brains, knock some sense into him," she said. Her words were followed by the sound of her hand slapping Bump upside the head.

"Ow, Skeet! That hurt!"

"Maybe if'n you was lookin' after yo' cousin—"

"Please, Miss Skeet, don't hit the boy again," Lone Wolf said. "There seems to be only so much sense that you are knocking into him."

Pee Wee snickered. Cousin Skeet did like whacking Bump upside the head, and Pee Wee liked to watch him flinch.

"If ya don't quit hittin' me, I'm goin' home," Bump said.

"This Junior, what she look like?" Aunt Teddy asked.

Pee Wee walked into the living room, interrupting. "Y'know somebody named 'Creole Kate'? That's her mama. They call her Junior on account she named after her. She a mixed girl, a little shorter than me."

Aunt Teddy frowned. "I know Creole Kate. She's always wanted to one-up me so she can be the only rootworker in town. But I'm not gonna let her bring that Voodoo in here and take my place."

Skeet walked over and patted Pee Wee on the head. "How you feelin', baby?"

"I'm all right, I guess. I just don't know what she did to me. She had somethin' in her hand, like a poppet, and she was laughin' all wicked-like. The poppet had my hair."

Aunt Teddy's eyes narrowed.

"She wanted me to practice some Voodoo with her," Pee Wee added. She accepted a glass of water from Lone Wolf and drank.

"How do you feel?" Lone Wolf asked.

"My stomach still hurts. My head hurts, too."

Lone Wolf looked into her eyes and nodded. He reached up and touched the top of her head. Pee Wee liked when he did this because his hands were big and warm, and he always smelled real nice, too.

"I can fix this," Lone Wolf said. "But I must leave for a while. I'll be back soon." He headed to the door.

"Hey!" Aunt Teddy said. "Where you think you're goin' in such a rush?"

"I can take this off Pee Wee, but I need to get some things first."

Pee Wee looked around. "Whatchu mean by that?"

"He's gonna remove the hex that's been put on ya, baby. Gonna uncross you." Aunt Teddy looked at Lone Wolf, "Never seen you use Injun magic before. Whatchu gettin'?"

"Sweet grass. I have some at my place."

Aunt Teddy huffed and pushed past Lone Wolf on her way into the kitchen. "Don't bother. I can undo this with just an egg and a bowl of water."

"Can someone please just uncross me already?" Pee Wee interjected. She doubled over as though she was going to vomit again. It sounded like she wanted to be sick, but there was nothing in her stomach to heave up.

"She outside!" Bump exclaimed. He pointed to the window and ran out onto the porch. "Junior is out by the chickens!"

Aunt Teddy ran out and saw a little girl with red hair doubled over, giggling and poking something in her hand. She was poking the poppet. And that poppet had Pee Wee's hair inside of it.

"I'll get her," Bump growled.

Pee Wee heard a voice whisper in her head. It was the voice of Viola. *"Come to my house, child. I'll help you deal with this little wench."*

Pee Wee slid out the back door as chaos erupted around her: Lone Wolf climbing down the front ladder, Aunt Teddy hollering orders, Cousin Skeet cackling in her rocking chair, and Bump stumbling over himself to get to Junior.

Shoeless, and wearing a long, shapeless black dress, Pee Wee followed the well-worn path back to her old house. Back to Viola's place.

INSIDE VIOLA'S HOUSE, the Voodoo woman's voice swirled around Pee Wee.

"I see the injun doin' somethin'. I think he's tryin' to get that girl's hair," it said.

Pee Wee sat in the center of some circles and squiggly lines drawn on the wood floor. Viola called them *veves*, but Pee Wee knew they were some kind of summoning spell for something. Each veve had a different shape and purpose. The one she sat on allowed her to speak with Viola, and she drew another veve to conjure something for the woman.

Evening beams of sunlight cast shadows through the broken and burned windows of what remained of the old house. Pee Wee drew the conjure veve because she didn't want to light the candles again and give away her location. No one could know she was here.

Pee Wee heard something running up outside, and Viola faded into a dark corner as Pee Wee walked over to where the door of Viola's house would be and hung a dark curtain there. She pulled the curtain back.

Bump stood in the doorway, breathless and holding a clump of something.

"Bump? Whatchu doin' here? How—"

"I followed you. Here, take this," The scent of butcher blood wafted off his clothes as he thrusted whatever it was he held at Pee Wee.

Pee Wee looked at the thing in his hand. "Did ya scalp somebody, Bump?"

"I got a braid of Junior's hair." Bump raised his hand and dangled the lock in front of Pee Wee.

"How ya get this?" She reached out to take it.

"Don't matter. Can you put a protection spell on me?

Cuz that was hard to come by, and I might have some people after me now." Bump looked around nervously, like he was waiting for someone to jump out of the bushes and attack.

Viola whispered to Pee Wee that a protection spell was possible, but that they needed to get to work on the hair first.

"Sure, sure."

"Teddy's powerful worried 'bout ya," Bump said. "She doesn't like you comin' out to this place. Says it's—"

"I come here to practice my rootwork, that's all. Now get gone. Let me do what I gotta do."

Bump looked Pee Wee up and down before he turned and ran down the path.

After Bump was out of sight, Pee Wee pulled the curtain back and returned to the circle.

"Not gonna need that conjure veve," Viola's voice said from the darkest corner of the room. "Wipe it down the middle to break it."

Pee Wee fingered the lock of Junior's reddish-colored hair. A bright red bow was tied to one end. She broke the veve like Viola said to.

"Now get to makin' the Voodoo doll."

Viola's wisp of a spirit body walked around Pee Wee as the girl worked hard on the Voodoo doll. She sewed some of Junior's hair onto the doll's head and stuffed the rest inside. Pee Wee prided herself on sewing, and she finished the doll before sunset. She held it up to show Viola.

"Good work. Now time to go get the poppet from Junior," Viola said. "Creole Kate works with the brothel girls. She protects that house, and I'm sure Junior sleeps there, too. You gotta get that doll she made of ya and bury it."

"Can't you just conjure the doll here?" Pee Wee pointed at the half-struck veve.

Viola paused. "I'm not real, child. I can't conjure much of nothin'."

"But how am I gonna get in that place? They goin' to be lookin' for me." Pee Wee stretched her arms behind her and arched her back to look up at the night sky through a hole in the roof. Her brain was running hot, and it felt like she was going to explode. "Can you tell me what the doll looks like, at least? I can make a copy and fool her into thinkin' I stole it from her already. Then Bump can sneak inside the brothel and take the real one."

Pee Wee wasn't sure, but it looked like Viola faded away for a bit before returning back to her spectral self. "Yes, I can," she said.

THE NEXT MORNING, Pee Wee stood outside the brothel where Junior and her mother lived. Bump ran around back while Pee Wee yelled taunts from the sidewalk.

Several of the brothel workers came to the front windows to see Pee Wee driving away their customers.

"Hey y'all! I hear that these ladies got some kinda crabs in they cooch! You don't wanna go in there unless ya wanna itch! Ain't that right, Junior?"

On of the brothel workers yelled down from the window, "Who told you that?"

Pee Wee cupped her hands to her mouth and yelled, "Don't matter! I hear one time Junior wet the bed, and her mama hung the sheets out back to dry without even washin' 'em first. Then they just put 'em on somebody else's bed and didn't tell no one!"

Creole Kate came to the window and yelled down, "Whatchu doin' here, Pee Wee? Ain't Teddy got somebody's root to steal?"

"She say *you* stole *her* root! That's why your spells don't work. I hear somebody got the clap in there! I hear it's the mayor's favorite girl. Or is it the sheriff's?"

Junior opened the front door to the brothel and glared at Pee Wee. Her hair was now cut short on both sides. "Whatchu want, Pee Wee?"

"I don't want nothin.' I want you to see what I got!" Pee Wee raised the Voodoo doll in the air and pulled a pin out of her pocket. "See this? Sure looks like your hair, don't it? All lopsided, like a blind man cut it!"

Junior touched her snipped locks. Her eyes filled with tears. "You sent your cousin to cut my hair, didn't you?"

"Don't matter! You done put somethin' on me, and I want it gone!" Pee Wee stabbed the doll in the stomach, and Junior doubled over. "I ain't got nothin' else to do, so I can stand here all day!"

Junior glared at Pee Wee.

Pee Wee laughed and made a big production out of putting the Junior doll in her bag and rifling around inside the bag before pulling out a different doll, one that looked like her—the Pee Wee doll.

"How'd you get that?" Junior screamed, and ran down the stairs toward Pee Wee. "You been in my room? How you get that?"

On Pee Wee's signal, a boy who had been standing off to the side, tryin' to act all ordinary, nodded his head at Bump, who had been hiding out of sight from Junior and Pee Wee. On the signal from the boy, Bump scampered into the building through the back door. Once inside, he went around until he found Junior's room and tore the place apart when he arrived. All the while, Pee Wee and

Junior fought outside in the street, with Pee Wee yellin' vulgar taunts the entire time.

"These girls all got the clap and crabs! If'n you want some good girls, y'all go see Miss Kitty's place on Rue Salle! At least there, y'all go home with your man-meat still fresh!"

Junior tried to hit Pee Wee in the face but missed, which allowed Pee Wee a clean jab to Junior's eye."

"This ain't what I wanted, Pee Wee!"

"Girl, if you don't shut your mouth, I'll shut it for ya! Don't y'know my sisters beat my ass all the time? That's how I keep beatin' yours!" Pee Wee tagged Junior again before she swept the girl's leg out from beneath her. Junior fell hard onto her back, legs in the air and dress raised to reveal that she wasn't wearing any bloomers.

"No wonder ya stink so bad!" Pee Wee waved her hand in front of her face, pretending to smell something foul.

When Pee Wee looked up, she saw Bump exit the house in a hurry and race down the street, and she turned to follow him.

Pee Wee yelled over her shoulder as she ran, "Remember ya'll! Go to Miss Kitty's! Not this one! Too much bad Voodoo here!"

She caught up with Bump, and they ran into the woods at the end of the road, where they waited for Junior to come running along after them.

Bump kneeled down in some bushes next to Pee Wee. "You think she gonna come?"

"Her or her mama. One of 'em, for certain."

Moments later, Junior came running with her mother into the woods.

Pee Wee took the doll from Bump and stood where Junior and her mother could see her.

"You done me wrong, Junior! You done me wrong with

this doll!" Pee Wee held it up in the air. "Now, I'm gonna do you right!" Pee Wee tossed the doll to Bump and pulled out the doll she made of Junior.

"Pee Wee, no! I'm sorry!" Junior screeched.

Creole Kate smacked Junior in the head. "You made a doll of that girl? She done nothin' to you, and you made a doll of her?"

"But Mama, I wanted to be like you. You said that her aunt—"

Creole Kate was a huge woman with arms and legs like tree stumps. She had a shock of red hair that burned like fire at its hottest. Her face was nothing but freckles, pale skin, and a nose that looked broken one too many times. "Grown-folk-business stay between grown folks. You make amends to this girl!" Creole Kate pushed Junior to the ground. "Do it or don't come back!"

Junior looked up at her mother, tears streaking her face, "I just wanted—"

"You make amends!" Creole Kate turned to Pee Wee and uttered an apology. "I'm sorry she did that to you, Pee Wee. I gots nothing against ya." And with that, she headed back to the brothel by herself.

Still kneeling on the ground, Junior looked up at Pee Wee and growled an apology.

Pee Wee ignored Junior. Instead, she spoke to the doll that resembled Junior. "I have made you, and your name is Junior," Pee Wee said to the doll. "You shall now receive the negative energy sent to me by Junior." Pee Wee wrapped a ribbon around the doll, then added, "I bind you from doin' harm. I bind you from doin' any rootwork against me or my family. I bind you, Junior, from doin' *anyone* harm."

The real Junior wobbled to her feet and held her hand out, trying to stop Pee Wee from finishing the spell. "Don't do that. It's the only thing I got."

Pee Wee stepped backward and repeated the lines, "I bind you from harming yourself and from doing harm to others. I bind you, Creole Kate Junior."

Junior struggled to take a step forward and fell. She pleaded with Pee Wee, but Pee Wee spoke the spell over and over as she continued to back away.

Once at a distance, Pee Wee lit a match and set the doll on fire, then dropped the flaming poppet into a hole. "Junior, don't you never harm nobody again." She then kicked some dirt into the hole to cover the doll and snuff out the flame. When she looked up, she saw Junior lying face-down on the ground.

"What'd you do?" Bump asked.

"Go look," Pee Wee said.

Bump ran over to Junior and flipped her onto her back. When he looked back at Pee Wee, his face had lost all its color. He climbed shakily to his feet and ran to her, whispering under his breath, "You can't do somethin' like that. You can't do that, Pee Wee."

She smirked and walked away.

"How could you do that, Hattie Mae? How could you do that?" Bump yelled and pointed back at Junior. "You done burnt her face! You burned her, Pee Wee! Why?"

Pee Wee stopped walking. "I done told y'all I'm dangerous. I'm gonna be the best damned conjure woman ever, and ain't no one gonna stop me. Don't believe me? Mess around and find out. She lucky I ain't take her mama's power, too."

Bump stopped, waited until Pee Wee turned to face him.

"You comin'?" Pee Wee asked.

"I ain't never seen you act like this before."

Pee Wee walked back to Bump. Once in front of him, she removed her hand from the conjure bag at her hip and opened her palm to reveal a small pile of powder. She blew the powder in Bump's face and tapped him on the forehead, telling him to forget.

"Now you ain't gotta remember it," she said. She laughed as she watched him close and reopen his eyes, then shake the cobwebs from his head.

"Pee Wee? Where… Where are we? What are we doin' out here?"

"We out here gatherin' stuff for Aunt Teddy. Don't you remember?"

"Oh. No, I guess I don't."

She grabbed his arm and pulled him toward the street. "Well, no need to worry. We got what we came for. Now let's get back to Aunt Teddy's before she starts to worry."

After Pee Wee and Bump disappeared down the street, Lone Wolf stepped out from his hiding place behind a tree and ran over to Junior to look at her face.

Her skin was burned. Her eyes were cloudy.

He helped Junior sit up and made a salve to put over her eyes. He ripped a piece of her ragged potato-sack dress and tied it around her head. "You'll be all right." He walked over to where Pee Wee buried the doll and dug at the ground, but the doll wasn't there, and he felt like something was watching him from the woods.

"Where did it go?" he asked himself.

A voice whispered on the wind, *"Not your problem."*

He stood, fixed the uncovered dirt with his boot, and headed back to Aunt Teddy's. She needed to know about this. She needed to know that her niece was becoming dangerous.

WHITE TENT REVIVAL

…as told by Pee Wee

I WAS WALKIN' the path back to Aunt Teddy's house one day when I saw another Injun headed towards Lone Wolf's place. This Injun looked like Lone Wolf, but he seemed like he didn't live near the city. He had feathers 'round his head and rode a horse without a saddle. I remember when Betty tried to get me to ride a horse without a saddle. I did, and I thought my stuff was gonna be sore forever. But this Injun was ridin' so fast that he was a black streak when he shot past me.

Aunt Teddy stood at the top of the path, towelin' her sweaty forehead.

"Who's that headin' to see Mista Wolf?" I asked.

"Come on, Pee Wee, we gotta head into town to get some lemons."

This was her nice way of tellin' me to shut my mouth and mind my own.

While we walked, Aunt Teddy didn't say much. She just held her hand over her stomach and looked like she was gonna fall down any minute. I stopped and picked some mint leaves off the path and ran to a nearby creek to wash 'em. When I returned, I gave 'em to Aunt Teddy to help with her pains.

She nodded and shoved the entire bunch into her mouth, chewed them leaves as hard as she could. I knew what was goin' on even though she hadn't told me. She was pregnant, and I had a good idea who the father was.

"So, when ya gonna tell me 'bout you and Mista Wolf?" I asked, kickin' at the dirt path.

"Ain't nothin' to tell."

"I ain't stupid, Aunt Teddy. You gonna have to tell me sometime before you start showin'." I made a big motion over my stomach like a balloon and waddled like I was pregnant.

"Ain't no such thing—" she started, then stopped walkin' and sighed. "Fine, Pee Wee. Yes, I'm pregnant. How'd y'know?"

"When y'all ready to believe I'm gonna be one of the best conjure women ever? I got conjure-woman intuition."

"Hmm." Aunt Teddy started walkin' down the path again.

I decided to answer serious. "Mista Wolf brings you fruits and vegetables, catches rabbits and a possum for ya. He even made you some stew, and I saw when you threw it right up. You said that you couldn't eat nothin' with a smell like that. That only means one thing."

Aunt Teddy chuckled. "The Great and Powerful Pee Wee," she grumbled.

"Make fun of me all you want," I said, "but when I gots the whole town on they knees needin' me, we'll see who's laughin' then."

We got a bunch lemons and some other stuff at the store and carried it all home. When we got back, Lone Wolf was sittin' on the step with his Injun friend, waitin' for us.

"Where have you been?" he asked Aunt Teddy.

"Went to the store." Teddy looked at the other man. "Who's this?"

"A friend of mine from a long time ago. Teddy, he found my sister." Lone Wolf looked at Aunt Teddy in a serious way.

"She okay?"

I was just standin' there, holdin' the bag of groceries, lookin' real stupid, so I decided to introduce myself to the new man. "Hello, my name is Hattie Mae, but you may call me Miss Conway." I swung the bag of groceries over to my hip and extended my hand for a shake.

The Injun stood and looked at my hand before shakin' it. He was barely as tall as I was, which wasn't a lot, and he was real skinny, like he could use a good meal or two. I knew this because he wasn't wearin' a shirt and his ribs were showin'. If only I had my mama's cornbread and some greens, I coulda got him nice and fat.

"Running Bear," he said.

"Hmm. You such a little thing. Maybe Little Running Cub would be better."

He laughed and took the bag of groceries from me after asking very polite-like if he could help. I said it was fine and led him into the house.

"Mista Bear," I said as I unpacked the bag.

"Um, Running Bear is fine, Miss Conway."

I laughed at the way he called me Miss Conway. I *liked* Miss Conway. "You want some water?" I grabbed a glass and filled it with water from a pitcher. "You talk real good for an Injun," I said, givin' him the water.

"I had some schooling, Miss Conway."

I looked again at his skinny chest. "I'd feel more comfortable if you had a shirt on," I said.

Before Running Bear could respond, Aunt Teddy came stompin' up the stairs all heated, and Lone Wolf followed.

"If I don't go get her soon, I don't know what will happen," Lone Wolf was saying to Aunt Teddy. "Tomorrow, the whole town will be at the revival, so it will be easy for me to sneak into the jail and get her."

Aunt Teddy got to work in the kitchen. Lone Wolf talked the entire time.

I took Running Bear outside to show him the enclosed porch. I pointed to the couch there, but instead of takin' a seat, he walked over to the screen and looked out. He made a clickin' sound with his mouth, and I saw his horse look up at him from the water trough below.

"I didn't know Mista Wolf had a sister," I said. "What's goin' on with her? She in trouble?"

"She's in jail, in a town down river by the name of Luton. It's a very dangerous town. I go there sometimes to trade, but I don't stay long when I do."

"Why not? Whatchu mean by dangerous?"

"It's dangerous for people like you and me, Miss Conway."

"People like us?"

"Black. Brown. Anything but white. If they catch people like us in their town after sundown…" Running Bear's voice trailed off.

"What was Mista Wolf's sister doin' there then? She's an Injun, too, ain't she? Didn't she know she wasn't welcome?"

"A white man invited her there, wanted her for his own, but when she rejected his proposal, she was beaten badly by the man and his friends and tossed in jail to await punishment."

Pa used to tell us girls stories about hidin' in the woods at night because some towns wouldn't let him walk through after sundown, but I always thought the stories were just more of Pa's tall tales. Almost everyone got along in our parish, and no one was expected to leave town before sunset.

A loud crash came from the kitchen as Lone Wolf joined us on the porch. "We leave tomorrow," he said to Running

Bear. "Let's go." His voice was colder than I had ever heard before.

Aunt Teddy stepped out behind him. I knew she was angry cuz I felt her anger before I saw her. It slapped me in the face. Even Running Bear took a step back.

"You'll be doin' no such thing, Wolf!" Aunt Teddy said.

"She's my sister," Lone Wolf said through gritted teeth. "We leave in the morning."

Aunt Teddy looked at me, studied me with her eyes. "You're taking Pee Wee with ya then. I won't have you goin' alone with this Running Bear fella I never met." She glared at Running Bear.

"Me?" I said. "Whatchu want me to do?"

Aunt Teddy didn't answer. She just stomped off to her bedroom and retired for the night.

I WOKE THE next morning when Aunt Teddy flopped down on my bed next to me. I hadn't slept much that night and somehow felt more exhausted than when I went to bed.

Aunt Teddy set a cup of coffee and some biscuits on my nightstand. "Make sure he gets back here with his sister," she said to me. "Now eat up. You're gonna need the energy. I'm gonna go pack some more food for the trip." She got up and headed for the kitchen.

"Are you okay?" I asked.

She stopped at my bedroom door but continued on without answerin'.

A short while later, Lone Wolf returned with Running Bear to make good on their promise to take me along.

They both rode sleek, black horses. After Aunt Teddy packed two days' worth of food, she pulled Lone Wolf aside to talk in private. I stayed near the horses with Running Bear.

"How far is Luton?" I asked.

Running Bear adjusted his horse's saddle. "A half day's ride."

"Do you think this is a good idea?"

"No, but Lone Wolf is my friend. Besides, I'm the only one who's been to the town. He needs a guide."

I fixed a scarf around my head to cover my long black plaits. Aunt Teddy thought it would be a good idea if'n I wore pants and tried to hide that I was a girl. I also brought my conjure bag, filled with some charms and powders, just in case we found ourselves in a precarious situation, and I needed to do some rootwork to get us out.

Lone Wolf returned. "Pee Wee will ride with me," he said.

Aunt Teddy walked over with some food wrapped in paper and cloth, and gave it to Lone Wolf, who stuffed the food into one of his horse's saddlebags.

I mounted the horse with his help.

"No," he said, once I was on the saddle. "You sit in front."

I scooted forward until I was pressed against the saddle's horn.

"This is gonna be hell on my cooch," I grumbled.

Aunt Teddy slapped my leg in disgust and scolded me for my foul language.

Running Bear carried two huge bows and handed one to Lone Wolf. The Lone Wolf I knew was always takin' care of animals and bein' kind to people. I couldn't imagine him with a weapon. Then again, I'd never seen him when his sister's life was at stake.

I understood that kind of anger. It was the same anger I felt toward the sheriff who killed my pa. His family, too. When I saw his wife about town, I wanted to do my worst to her, but lucky for me, Lone Wolf was with me and helped calm me down before I gone and did somthin' stupid.

"Pee Wee, let God deal with her. You are not God," he'd whispered.

"My pa is dead, and you sayin' to let God deal with her?"

"Everything will right itself in the universe," he'd said.

"You talk in riddles, I swear."

"Trust me."

A little Black girl, smaller than me, ran behind that sheriff's wife, holdin' the woman's bags.

"That look like the universe rightin' itself?" I'd said, pointin' to the servant girl.

Lone Wolf never replied.

I'd lost track of how long we'd been ridin', but I reckoned that Running Bear and Lone Wolf were powerful hot by the way they was sweatin'.

Lone Wolf finally slowed his horse to a stop. "We'll stop here for a bit," he said to Running Bear. "Let the horses get some water."

"Good, cuz I gotta go relieve myself," I said.

Lone Wolf cleared his throat. "Pee Wee, I didn't know you were awake. I thought you'd fallen asleep."

"I was thinkin' about stuff. About Pa. About bein' angry. See, I know why you's angry about your sister. I know what that feels like."

I climbed down off the horse with Lone Wolf's help and ran behind some bushes. I didn't realize how bad I had to go until I squatted down and let loose.

While doin' my business, I remembered how Aunt Teddy used to make my sisters and I pee in buckets. Made us carry them buckets everywhere. Said that our pee was a lifesaver. Now all that life-savin' pee was slidin' down into a hole in the ground behind me, and I couldn't be more relieved.

When I finished, I joined Lone Wolf and Running Bear beneath a nearby tree. Running Bear tossed me a wet cloth to wipe my hands clean, then spread the contents of the food bag out on the ground for the three of us to share. Lone Wolf sat against the tree and ran his finger over a map.

"Map says we're close. Just over those hills and we'll be there."

Running Bear nodded. "Yes, but we'll have to leave the horses here. We'll need to sneak into town on foot."

Somethin' about this didn't sit well with me.

"I think I'll stay with the horses," I said.

They both looked at me.

"No, you'll come with us," said Lone Wolf. "I promised Teddy I wouldn't let you out of my sight."

"I'm more than capable of takin' care of myself, thank you," I said.

Lone Wolf tried to get clever: "Yes, but what if we need your Hoodoo magic?"

"You got bows and arrows, don't ya? Other weapons, too, I see." I pointed at a sharpened tomahawk fastened to Running Bear's belt. "Hand me that hatchet, will ya?"

"Why?"

"You'll see."

Running Bear pulled the tomahawk from his belt and handed me the weapon. From my bag, I retrieved some rope and looped it around the tomahawk's handle, tied one end tight.

"Here, Mista Wolf," I said, handin' the new tomahawk to him. "Try it now."

Lone Wolf took the rope and used it to swing the tomahawk in a circle above his head. He aimed for a nearby tree and let it loose like a rope dart, still holdin' on to the free end of the rope like it were nothin' more than a kite string. The sound of the tomahawk hittin' the tree trunk made a loud *thunk* noise, which made Lone Wolf smile. He then yanked on the rope to pull the bladed weapon free from the trunk and dragged it back to him, hand over hand, like he was pullin' in a fishin' net.

"Not bad for a beginner," I said, applaudin' his technique. "Not as good as me, but you'll get better."

Lone Wolf and Running Bear shared a smile.

From our shared feast, I grabbed a handful of sweet berries that had some sprinkles of mint on top, then started munchin' away.

"Like I was sayin', you have plenty of weapons between the two of yous. I'll stay here with the horses."

"You will come with us," Lone Wolf said. "Now, eat well. This will be our last meal before heading into town."

That's when I noticed the ham that Aunt Teddy had packed. We only got ham in times of trouble. In case it was our last meal, Aunt Teddy wanted it to be a good one. The ham was a bad omen, in my mind, but it smelled so good with that sweet glaze on top of it, and I couldn't resist. Even the bees buzzed about us, hopin' to get some of that glaze for theyselves.

After our feast, I felt relaxed enough to take a nice, long nap right there 'neath that tree, but Lone Wolf kept pacin' back and forth all nervous-like, which made me nervous, too.

"You jumpier than a cat in a hot skillet," I said.

He stopped and stared at me for a bit, smiled, then kept on pacin'.

Eventually I fell asleep to the memory of catchin' catfish with my sisters and Pa. Ma was there, too, smokin' her pipe and laughin'. No Bump, no Cousin Skeet, just my sisters, parents, and me. Ma fried up the fish and served it to us girls, and even in the dream, I could smell every spice, feel all the grease on my fingers, taste every juicy morsel on my tongue. It was heavenly. Pa started a fire and threw somethin' that smelled like sweet earth on top of it so that the bugs would stay away. We stayed out there, just the five of us, until the sun started settin'. Then, stupid Betty came over to wake me up.

"Pee Wee, ya gotta go," she said.

"I don't wanna. Why can't we stay here?"

"Because you gotta help Lone Wolf save his sister. I'll see you soon." She kissed me on the forehead, and I awoke.

I opened my eyes to see Lone Wolf kneelin' over me, with his hand on my shoulder. "Sounds like you were dreaming of your family."

"I really miss my sisters. And my pa."

He made a small sound like a sigh, then told me that we needed to leave.

I nodded and looked around. The sun was settin' and Running Bear was tendin' to the horses. Both he and Lone Wolf had changed clothes, and their faces had been painted with war paint. They looked real scary. My heart pounded in my chest like those drums they played at my pa's funeral.

THE TENT FOR the revival was the biggest thing of its kind I ever saw. There was even a wood floor on the inside. Outside the tent, a buncha men roasted pigs while the women set the dinner tables. Children ran about, playin' whatever games white kids played. The roasted pig smelled burnt and without flavor. I remember thinkin' to myself that those men needed to put some spices on the animal—or somethin' in the fire. I wondered if'n they even had a skillet for some cornbread.

My heart pounded somethin' terrible as we quietly approached the tent in the dark. When we got close enough, we hid in the bushes and watched as one of the men silenced the crowd and began to speak.

"Welcome, my brothers and sisters, to the resurrection! We are here to speak in tongues and speak the name of our lord and savior Jesus Christ! We ask for the Heavenly Father to bless us all! Lay your hands on us Lord and bless us in your name!"

Another man started yellin' like it was the end of the world, but he didn't sound like no preacher I grew up with. When our preachers told us it was the end of the world, we believed 'em. One time as a little girl, I even ran out the tent and cried because I thought fire was gonna rain down from the sky and Satan was 'bout to rise from the earth and get us.

"Are you saved? Have you asked for forgiveness from Jesus? Accepted him into your heart as your one true lord and savior?"

A sweaty man at the front of the crowd thumped his Bible while lookin' around for suspicious people in the crowd.

A preacher-man once tried to tell Bump that he wasn't saved, but that didn't end well for him. Cousin Skeet was so angered by the man's words, she got right up in his face and put the fear of God—and maybe even the devil—in him.

> *"I seen ya runnin' from that young gal's house down by the levy!"* she had shouted, shakin' her cane at the preacher. She took that cane and whacked him in the head with it. *"Don't tell me that my boy ain't saved! He saved! Now get yo' snake oil outta this town, ya damned charlatan!"*

The white people in the revival tent started wavin' paper fans and yelling, "Amen!" There were even some screams and faintin', I guess. But it all sounded real phony to me.

After most of the crowd had filtered into the tent, Running Bear pointed us toward the town, and we went.

The town was small, only a few buildings here and there, and the only one with a light on just happened to be the jail.

From our hidin' spot in the alley across the way, I watched Lone Wolf aim his bow and arrow, take a deep breath, and loose that bolt toward the jail. It made a sound like *thwoosh* as it flew through the air and into an open window, where it struck the man inside, killin' him.

Lone Wolf ran across the road and looked inside to confirm the man was dead before motionin' for Running Bear and myself to leave our hidin' spot and join him.

We ran over and followed him into the jailhouse.

Inside, a man's legs were in the air, and the back of his chair was flat on the ground. I tried to look and see where the arrow had pierced him, but Lone Wolf stood in front of me while Running Bear ran over to the body to retrieve the arrow. I couldn't see much of anythin', but I heard him pullin' the arrow out, and I will never forget the sound.

They moved the dead man's body up against a wall behind the desk and set the chair up straight. Lone Wolf removed the ring of keys from the man's belt and ran to the back where the jail cell was.

I followed him and watched as his sister reached for him through the cell bars. "Brother!" she whispered and grabbed at him.

Lone Wolf ran over and pressed his forehead to hers, pulled back to look at her. His sister's long hair was barely shoulder length now, and it looked like someone had taken no care when choppin' it off with a knife. The ends were all blunt and uneven.

"Where is your hair?" he asked. The pain was apparent in his voice. "It was so beautiful." He ran his fingers through what was left of her dark locks.

"They cut it because the lady of the house thought I was prettier than her."

Gettin' a good look at her now, I could see that Lone Wolf's sister was just a tinier, more feminine version of him. Her shirt was too big, and her skirt dragged across the floor when she walked, but she was so pretty that it didn't much matter what her clothes looked like, honestly. Her skin was so smooth and brown. The only blemish was the nasty black eye from when someone must've socked her.

I looked inside her cell. No bed or toilet, just a bucket for relievin' oneself and some straw to sleep on. There was a single window in the back of the cell with bars on it, but I figured that must be hell when it rained. Somethin' in the shadows seemed to move, but I couldn't make out what it was.

Lone Wolf did a quick introduction while he used the keys to unlock the cell door. "Sister, this is Pee Wee. And you know Running Bear. Pee Wee, this is my sister Aiyana Olathe." With a *click*, the door unlocked, and he swung it open. "Let's go," he whispered.

Aiyana Olathe exited the cell and hugged him tight. "Brother, we need to take her with us."

"Who?"

I had seen the woman before Lone Wolf's sister pointed to her, hidin' there in the back of the cell where I'd seen somethin' move. I just hadn't said anythin' 'bout her because I thought she was a ghost, judgin' by the size and paleness of her. She was the tiniest white woman I had ever seen, and she had the reddest hair that looked like fire. She ran over to the door and reached for Aiyana Olathe.

"You say…*me?*" She pointed to herself. "*Mo mhac! Mo mhac!*" Her accent was so heavy and strange, I could hardly understand her. She grabbed a reddish scarf and wrapped it around her shoulders. Her small feet were bare and gnarled like knots in a tree. She didn't bother puttin' on shoes, most likely cuz she didn't own any.

Together, the five of us ran outta the jailhouse, but before we got far, the white woman grabbed my wrist. She was scrawny but strong, and she smelled like Ma—fresh-baked bread, soap, and sunshine. The smell was intoxicatin', and I was bewitched.

"*Mo mhac!*" She touched my face, caressed my skin. "*Mo mhac!*" She then grabbed Running Bear's wrist as well, and dragged us off behind the jailhouse.

Running Bear whistled a signal to Lone Wolf, and Lone Wolf responded with a whistle that sounded like three quick whistles, and we were off with this very tiny white lady with hair that looked like fire.

She dragged us to a field, holdin' my wrist like my mama when I was in trouble. She kept sayin' those words—"*Mo mhac!*"—over and over again until finally I asked Running Bear if'n he knew what she was sayin'.

"I don't," he said. "She's not from here."

"Then where's she from?"

"I don't know. Are you sure we should be following her?"

"Yes. I feel it in my soul. Whatever she's sayin' and wherever she's takin' us must be real important."

We stopped behind a large barn and next to a locked door that opened to the inside. The woman reached up and pulled a pin from her hair, then started fiddlin' with the lock. I never felt so stupid just standin' outside a barn, as if waitin' to be captured, but 'fore long, the woman had picked that lock and opened the door for us to enter.

"You stay here," I whispered to Running Bear. "Keep watch. Let Mista Wolf know if somethin' bad happens to me."

Running Bear nodded.

Inside the barn, the moon shone down through an opening in the roof, down onto a bale of hay. The woman ran over to the bale, and I heard a chain rattle. Is she gonna steal a horse? We *could* use another one. But, no, it wasn't a horse. I knew because I saw a small foot on the floor, and it slid behind the bale.

The woman kneeled and stretched her arms out. From behind the bale emerged a small Black boy, wearing a pair of raggedy pants tied around his waist with a rope. He didn't have no shirt, and he had all these dark marks on his arms and back. Some of them was healed, but some of them was raw. He was hobbled by a chain clamped around his ankle, but even with that weight, that pain, he willed himself to move as fast as he could toward the woman, then threw his arms around her in a big, tearful hug. I knew then that she was somethin' special to him. Only one person in the whole world can make you forget your pain like that, can heal your wounds with they tears.

She was this boy's mama.

"*Mo mhac!* James. *Mo mhac!*" She covered his head with kisses, and he let her. She reached down and pulled some sort of salve from the folds of her greenish dress and rubbed it on the boy's ankle. Once the ankle bone was lubricated enough, she helped the boy slip his lil foot from the chain's hold. And once he was free, they hugged again.

She turned him around and rubbed the salve into the wounds on his back. He didn't flinch once. I would've been screamin' and hollerin' like somebody was tryin' to kill me, had I been made to suffer through somethin' like that, but that little boy just braced himself and let his mama rub that salve until she was done. I wanted to cry. I could never be that strong, even with Ma and Pa holdin' me down and promisin' that Jesus his self would take away my pain.

I knelt down beside the boy and looked into his small round face. Dried tears streaked his cheeks. "Your name James?" I asked.

"Yes'm."

"This your mama?"

"Yes'm. Her name is Eliza, and she's from a long ways away, far across the ocean. A place called *Errland*, or at least that's what she tol' me. They took me from her and made me work in a white man's house with some Injun lady. I missed her so much." James wrapped himself around her again.

"Eliza?" I said to the woman.

She smiled and nodded.

I then pointed to myself. "Pee Wee. *Pee. Wee.*"

That's when Running Bear opened the barn door and whispered to us from outside. "Miss Conway! Someone's coming!"

"Okay, okay," I mumbled to myself.

James, meanwhile, took his mama's hand and whispered, "Go! Go now!"

I heard Eliza snifflin' a bit and I knew she was cryin'. But she was smilin', too. She kept sayin' those same words over and over: "*Mo mhac!* James!"

Running Bear started runnin' back toward the jail, but Eliza grabbed him and pulled him in a different direction, pointin' to a thicket not so far away.

"We can't go that way!" Running Bear protested. "They'll see us!"

But it was too late. A loud bell started ringin'.

"They know we're here!" I said. "I'm goin' to the trees with Eliza."

I ran across that field like my butt was on fire, and soon, I heard Running Bear breathin' hard behind me, tryin' to catch up. Then I saw Running Bear in front of me, reachin' back to grab my hand and pull me into the trees before we was spotted.

Eliza motioned for us to head farther into the thicket "*Go raibh maith agaibh,*" she whispered.

"She says thank you," James said. "She will keep you safe."

He reached up to take his mama's hand, and she led us deeper into the woods.

"Where are we going?" Running Bear asked.

Eliza made a big circle with her arm to illustrate, whispered something in the language I couldn't understand.

"We're goin' around the town," James said.

Eliza looked down at James and smiled at him. She patted him lovingly on the head.

I thought back to what James said earlier, about where his mama was from.

"Hey Running Bear, you ever heard of a place called *Eerland*? That's where James says his ma is from."

Eliza must've heard me, cuz she tsked and shook her head, pronounced the name more slowly until I understood what she was tryin' to say.

"*Ireland*," I whispered. "You're from Ireland."

Eliza nodded, then put a finger to her lips to tell us all to hush. In the silence, we could hear the white folks searchin' about, lookin' for us. We heard the dogs.

I grabbed a small jar of black pepper from my conjure bag and sprinkled some on the ground.

Eliza looked at me, puzzled.

"For the dogs," I explained. "To cover our scent."

James translated, and his mother nodded her head in approval.

"We have to keep moving," Running Bear said.

But I just kept sprinklin' pepper. "I'm the best conjure woman to ever live. Ain't no dog in the world stands a chance against me and this here Hoodoo bag."

"Do you want to be hanged?" Running Bear shot back.

That's when I heard James's little voice in my ear: "Mama and Bridgid will protect us."

"Bridgid? Who's Bridgid?"

James laughed. "Bridgid's everywhere, Pee Wee."

The deeper Eliza led us into the trees, the more those trees felt alive, as if they was conscious and gatherin' together to protect what was left of 'em. Light danced through the openings in the canopy and made me think shadows had come to life and were runnin' alongside us through the forest. It smelled like perfumed wildflowers the farther we walked. We came across some small pools of water that smelled like somethin' had died in 'em, but we kept movin'. I ran my hands over the ridges of tree bark, hopin' to feel somethin', some kind of hint as to where we was goin' or how we could escape. Sometimes my hand came back wet with dew, sometimes sticky with sap.

Up ahead in a small clearing, James was standin' with his hands cupped together in front of him. He giggled and started walkin' toward me with his hands still cupped, as if he was holdin' somethin' precious that he couldn't wait to give me.

"Take this. It'll follow the light."

He uncupped his hands and dropped a little lightning bug into my palm. Before I could take much of a look at the bug, it took flight and did a little loop in the air before zippin' off.

Running Bear tapped me on the shoulder and pointed to where the little lightning bug had joined a whole chorus of them, all lit up and guidin' us through the dark.

James smiled at us. He knew the way ahead. I could tell by the way he walked. He knew this path like I knew the path to Aunt Teddy's.

Up ahead, Eliza fought with her shawl and continued to pull things out of hidden pockets or from secret leg bands beneath her dress. She let go of her skirt and stopped, then knelt in front of a small pool of water. She looked around for James and pointed to the ground next to her. James ran over with two handfuls of twigs and sticks. He piled 'em together on the ground and started rubbin' two of the sticks together until he had a spark. He dropped the spark into the pile to make a fire.

Eliza, meanwhile, glanced at the plants around her and plucked several herbs from their stems. With her bounty in hand, she got low to the ground and moved around the water like she was one of them dogs trackin' our scent.

"She do Hoodoo?" I asked James.

James grinned. "No. My mama's a witch."

Lookin' into the fire, Eliza wrapped a cord around the plants in her hand.

I could tell just by the smell that what she plucked was mint, sage, and purple basil.

Once wrapped, Eliza tossed the bundle onto the fire. She called me over and grabbed me by the wrist, moved me to a spot next to her along the water's edge. She made a circular motion with her arm, then lifted my arm and made a circular motion with it as well.

"Are you sayin' I should go 'round this way?" I made the same circular motion with my arm again.

Eliza nodded.

"But we'll never make it," I said. "We're too far from our horses. We'll never make it back without gettin' caught. We should hide 'til mornin.'"

I looked up to see burned bodies hangin' in the trees some twenty yard away, and in that moment, I felt somethin' inside me that I done never felt before. I felt the tree, a regular ol' tree, wantin' to die right there in its roots because of the burned bodies that swung from its tender branches. I covered my mouth so as to stop myself from bein' sick.

Eliza raised her hands and chanted, "*Bridgid! Bridgid, tha mi ag iarraidh ort do nighean a dhìon! Dìon do nigheanan! Dìon mo phiuthar!*"

James whispered, "She askin' that Bridgid protect you. She callin' you her sister."

Eliza rose up on her tip toes and chanted louder, "*Sgòthan sealladh na muinntir a thig gun iarraidh!*"

I looked to James to see if he was goin' to tell me what she said, but he just sat there and stared at her in awe, like he'd never seen her do anythin' like this before.

Whatever Eliza was sayin', she said it three times—I gathered that much—and I could tell her words had power.

White smoke seemed to roll across the water toward us. The winds whipped, rustlin' the branches and leaves and forest detritus all around us, and the frogs started croakin' faster and louder and with more urgency. Next, the water started lappin' at our feet and the smell of standin' freshwater smelled salty. The air grew heavy and humid, and I found it hard to breathe. The smoke, it felt like it was crawlin' into my lungs.

Running Bear clutched his throat. He felt the smoke inside him, too. His eyes widened, and I knew he was thinkin' the same thing as me: we made a giant mistake followin' this woman into the woods.

James ran over to Running Bear and me, handed each of us a little square of fabric. He pointed to a similar piece of fabric wrapped 'round his face, then pulled the fabric 'round my nose and mouth and knotted it behind my head. The fabric smelled like mint and somethin' else I couldn't place. I looked to Running Bear, worried he was still in trouble, but he must've been watchin' us cuz he was busy tyin' his own square of fabric 'round his face.

The more I breathed in the scents inside that mask, the less my heart pounded like a drum. I felt more and more relaxed until all my troubles faded and I couldn't hear nothin' goin' on around us 'sides the comfortin' sounds of the animals hidin' in those woods.

Eliza raised her hands high, then bent down and held them low as she continued the spell. She made a wide sweepin' motion from left to right to left, as if attemptin' to send the smoke back in the direction from where we came, and it worked. The smoke followed her command. It swirled about like whipped-up fog and soon covered everythin' in our path.

Eliza dropped her arms and started laughin'.

James ran over and stood beside her, then started copying her laugh.

Running Bear and I stayed still. I tapped his shoulder, and he turned his head to follow the fog. The fog was like a living thing now, movin' through the trees and underbrush of its own accord. It choked whatever was in its path.

I watched as a little bunny rabbit hopped into the fog, twitched its nose, and fell dead as a doornail right there on the spot. Since the fog didn't seem to affect me or Running Bear none, I walked over and squatted down to look at the sad corpse. What I saw was even more troublin'. The rabbit was turned inside out. All the organs were on the outside and all the fur was on the inside. But as much as it scared me, I wanted this magic. I needed it.

Next thing we heard was the screams of our pursuers from somewhere deep inside them trees and fog. We heard the sickly thuds of their bodies fallin' to the ground, and the chokin' gasps in their throats.

I looked back to see James and Eliza whirlin' their torsos in circles about their waists, sendin' more of that deadly fog our way. But before it swallowed us, the fog split around us and continued onward toward the farm, the jail, the town, the tent.

"Lone Wolf!" I exclaimed. "We have to warn him and his sister! The fog is headin' their way!"

I reached out and ran my fingers through the fog just to make sure it was safe for us to go. Nothin' happened.

"You won't get hurt," James said to us with a smile. "Ma protects you. Bridgid protects you. She protect all her children."

"I want to come back and learn!" I said.

James said somethin' to his mother, but she just waved him off with a sour look on her face. I knew what that look meant: "Not now, I'm busy!" Some languages are universal.

"I'll find you, James. And I will find you, Eliza."

I grabbed Running Bear and we turned back toward the fog. It was thick enough to cut with a knife, but somehow we could still see through it, so we ran. I could hear James laughin' behind us, and the sound moved all around us. It was in front of us, beside us, above us, and even beneath our feet. Running Bear and I ran fast, and we ran together, holdin' each others' hands tight. His hand was awful sweaty, but I didn't let go.

As we get closer to edge of the thicket, I heard them dogs again, but this time, they was cryin' out in pain. A shotgun blast rang out.

Sometime later, we arrived back at the horses to find Lone Wolf and his sister waitin' for us.

RUNNING BEAR LEFT our little town a few days after our heroic return from Luton. We never talked about our time with Eliza and James. Never talked about the fog. Never talked about the screams or the terrible things we saw.

One time when he came to visit, Running Bear and I snuck back into Luton to see if things had changed, but the entire town looked abandoned, like everyone had just up and ran away. The white tent still stood, but it looked older, and part of it was caved in, and other parts were overgrown with nature. We braved the inside of a few houses, but they was all empty of livin' things, save for some bats and other rodents that now lived inside the walls. More than a few ceilings had collapsed. Most of the wood had started to rot.

But even stranger was how the town smelled. Everywhere we went, it smelled sweet like fresh wildflowers. The same wildflowers from the woods.

Stranger still, for as long as we was in the town of Luton, James's laughter never left us.

THE HOUSE OF ILL REPUTE

PEE WEE SAT up in bed and listened to Aunt Teddy moving about the house. She heard bottles clanking together and things being pounded in bowls. What she didn't hear was the voice of Lone Wolf. He seemed to always lurk around the corner, or out in the yard with the pigs. But when Pee Wee kicked out of bed and walked out to the front porch, she didn't see him anywhere.

"I need ya to get washed up and dressed," said Aunt Teddy. "You 'n' me are goin' into town today to see some friends of mine."

Pee Wee wiped the sleep from her eyes. "Did you cook breakfast yet? I'm so hungry, and some biscuits would taste real nice—with some butter."

Aunt Teddy herded Pee Wee back to her bedroom so the girl could get ready for the day. "After you get dressed, you can come back and eat. Just don't eat too much. They's gonna feed us where we're going."

Pee Wee washed her face with warm water from a pitcher and basin and brushed her teeth. For her outfit, she pulled on a plain black dress, stockings, and her favorite well-worn ankle boots. For her hairdo, she pulled her thick curls back into a ponytail. Her hair had grown so much since Ma moved away, and Pee Wee wasn't fond of cutting it, so she'd been wearing it in a ponytail lately more days than not. After she wrapped her favorite black scarf around her hair, she took the basin of water and dumped it off the front porch.

Pee Wee took a seat at the kitchen table, and Aunt Teddy thrust a bowl of grits into her hands.

"Now eat up," Aunt Teddy said. "We goin' soon."

"But what about—"

"I didn't make any biscuits, Hattie Mae. Now eat before I haul you outta this house on an empty stomach."

"Yes'm," Pee Wee grumbled. She looked down into the bowl and stirred the sugar and the tiny pat of butter into the soupy grains. On days like this, Pee Wee's role was to remain silent and do whatever Aunt Teddy said.

While Pee Wee ate, Aunt Teddy finished packing her supplies. When Pee Wee finished eating, she went to her bedroom and grabbed her conjure bag and stuffed a few extra things inside. When she returned to the kitchen, she helped Aunt Teddy carry a box of bottled whiskey down the back steps.

Out back, Lone Wolf waited for them atop his horse and wagon, reigns in hand.

"Mornin', Mista Wolf." Pee Wee said. "I was wonderin' where you was at." She loaded the box of bottles into the back of the wagon, beside a box of perfumes, and hopped inside with them.

Aunt Teddy climbed into the front of the wagon and took her seat next to Lone Wolf. "Wolf," she said flatly.

Lone Wolf sighed, then made a clicking sound with his mouth, signaling for the horse to get moving. The horse obeyed and started its trot in the direction of the town, pulling the wagon behind it.

Aunt Teddy turned from her seat up front and pointed at the box of bottles next to Pee Wee. "Don't spill none of that, ya hear?"

"What if we's in an accident?"

"Then you save as many of them bottles as ya can."

"These bottles really more important than me?"

"Until you start earnin' this family money, yes. That's some mighty fine whiskey right there. Some of the best I ever made." Aunt Teddy turned back to face the front.

It was still early when they arrived at the city, but the streets were already alive with music and the sound of streetcars clanging up and down the roads. Vendors hawked their wares, and children ran up beside the wagon, begging for coins.

So many breakfast smells filled the air: fried potatoes, bacon, sweet pancakes. Pee Wee even sniffed some crawfish, which meant gumbo was already being made for lunchtime. Why Lone Wolf had taken the route that made her stomach growl extra loud and her mouth fill with drool was beyond her.

She recognized a few of the people and watched them mosey along. She also recognized a bakery or two. Lone Wolf didn't seem to be in any type of hurry, as the horse clip-clopped down the road, but even so, the wagon was still moving too fast for Pee Wee to jump off, run inside one of the bakeries, and grab something fine to eat. Instead, she pulled her scarf around her nose and closed her eyes tight, so as to block out any temptation.

When they arrived at their destination, the wagon slowed to a stop.

Pee Wee heard the sound of little feet running up to the wagon, and when she opened her eyes and sat up, she looked down at a group of kids, all dressed in hand-me-downs and rags, asking if they could help carry something inside.

"No!" Pee Wee snapped. "This here's my job! Get back!"

"Be nice," Aunt Teddy said through a fake smile and gritted teeth.

Pee Wee adjusted her tone. "Get back...*please.*"

The house they stopped at was a two-story southern plantation-style home with a veranda on each story, the roof supported by a row of handsome white columns that stretched all the way to the ground. The facade was a cream color with evergreen accents—recently painted by the looks of it—while the porch floorboards were painted red, so as to better hide the bloodstains from all the fights that often happened there.

According to one of the girl's who worked there—a young girl by the name of Violet—the men that frequented the house got angry whenever their girl wasn't around, or worse, if she was already with another man.

"We got tired of cleanin' up all the blood," she had explained to Pee Wee, "so we painted them floorboards red to save us some trouble."

With help from Lone Wolf, Pee Wee climbed down from the back of the wagon and unloaded the one box of bottled whiskey and the one box of bottled perfumes onto the sidewalk.

Aunt Teddy grabbed the box of perfumes and said to Pee Wee. "C'mon, Miss Hattie Mae. Let's go sell some love potions."

Pee grabbed the box of bottled whiskey and lifted it to her chest. "See ya, Mista Wolf," she said.

Lone Wolf cleared his throat. "Ahem...yes. See ya soon, Pee Wee." He looked around, uneasy, at the kids that circled him and the wagon.

"He don't like this place much, do he?" Pee Wee asked Aunt Teddy as they walked together toward the house.

"He's not fond of it, no. But it puts money in our pockets."

A pale woman with huge breasts and a blonde wig stepped out of the house and onto the porch to greet Aunt Teddy and Pee Wee. Her lips were painted red, drawn in the shape of a cupid's bow, and a black beauty mark was dotted next to her left eye, drawn there by an eyebrow pencil. She wore heavy purple eyeshadow.

"Well, Miss Kitty," Aunt Teddy greeted. "It's so glorious to see you on the Lord's day!" She leaned in and kissed the air next to both of Miss Kitty's cheeks.

Miss Kitty spoke in a high soprano voice "Theodora, my dear, you look as resplendent as *evah*." She beamed and kissed the air next to Aunt Teddy's cheeks.

It annoyed Pee Wee when people tried to be something they weren't. And Miss Kitty definitely was one to put on airs.

"And my little Hattie Mae! Welcome back!" Miss Kitty held her hands open toward Pee Wee.

"Yes'm," Pee Wee mumbled. She nodded and stepped back until Aunt Teddy elbowed her and pushed her back toward Miss Kitty. While kissing the air next to Miss Kitty's cheeks, Pee Wee almost choked on the scent of the woman's perfume. It smelled like a mix of sugar and gasoline, and it made her eyes water something terrible.

"Have you eaten breakfast yet?" Miss Kitty asked Pee Wee. "You're such a tiny little thing!" Without waiting for an answer, she turned to Aunt Teddy and pointed at the box she held. "Where are my manners? Allow me to take those heavy boxes off your hands." Miss Kitty called to the side of the house for help. "Boys!"

Within seconds, three boys no older than Pee Wee came running out from the side of the house and stopped in front of Miss Kitty. These must have been new boys, Pee Wee reasoned, because their clothes still looked nice—never been stained or torn from hard work.

"Take these boxes into the parlor for Miss Theodora and Miss Hattie Mae," Miss Kitty instructed. "Then tell the girls inside to put out some tea and cakes for our guests here." Her hands pointed this way and that as she spoke, wrists twirling about like she was conducting some kind of illicit orchestra.

One of the boys took the box from Pee Wee's hands. "Pardon me, miss—"

"Her name, young man, is Hattie Mae," snapped Miss Kitty.

"No it ain't!" Pee Wee replied. "Hattie Mae is my high-class name, and this place is *not* high-class." She turned back to the boy. "Name's Pee Wee."

"Hi, Pee Wee. My name's Alex."

Alex had a hard, muscled body, caramel skin, and green eyes like a cat. His hair was brown, and his smile made something inside Pee Wee snap. His teeth were too nice to be working in a place like this, she thought. She looked at the other two boys. They all looked identical.

"We're triplets." Alex said, as if reading her mind. "You hungry?"

"Whatchu mean?"

"We have scrambled eggs and warm biscuits cookin' in the kitchen. That's if'n you want more than just tea cakes. I can show you the way if you like."

"Can't," Pee Wee replied. "I'm here to help my aunt."

Alex smiled. "Maybe I'll see ya later then." He winked, then took the box inside. His brothers followed.

"This way, ladies," Miss Kitty said to Aunt Teddy and Pee Wee. She led them inside the house and to the parlor, where Aunt Teddy and Pee Wee took their seats on a striped sofa.

On the parlor walls were naked photographs of the women who worked for Miss Kitty. Many of the women were mixed race, but there were a few white ones, and they wore their hair in buns fastened to the back of their heads.

Miss Kitty took a seat across from her guests on a black wingback chair that stood tall and straight, then whipped out a paper fan from somewhere inside her garments and started fanning herself something fierce.

"The portraits advertise the kind of girls we have here," she explained. "A nice young man came through and took them photos for free. It would've been quite expensive otherwise."

A girl not much older than Pee Wee entered the parlor holding a platter of tea and cakes, just as Miss Kitty promised. Pee Wee looked at the loose ringlets around the girl's caramel-colored face, at her emerald-green eyes, and thought she was rather pretty.

What's a girl like that workin' in a place like this? she wondered. *This can't be the best she can do, can it?*

"You like the photographs, don't you, Fabienne?" Miss Kitty said to the girl.

"Yes'm," Fabienne answered as she handed Pee Wee a steaming cup and saucer.

"Two sugar," Pee Wee said.

Fabienne dropped two cubes of sugar into Pee Wee's cup of tea and handed her a tiny spoon for stirring.

"Beignet?" she asked.

"Please." Pee Wee reminded herself of what Aunt Teddy had told her about eating in public—that she needed to eat with small, delicate bites, like a lady—but her growling stomach couldn't be tamed. She scarfed the beignet in two ravenous bites and washed the morsels down with a loud chugging of her tea. "More, please," she said after emptying the cup. She could feel Aunt Teddy's disapproving glare, but in the moment, she didn't care. Those beignets were too delicious to mind.

Fabienne giggled as she placed another beignet on a napkin and handed it over to Pee Wee. But when she looked into Pee Wee's face, she gasped.

"Fabienne!" Miss Kitty snapped. "Don't be rude!"

Pee Wee's brow furrowed. "Yeah!" she said, suddenly feeling quite defensive and self-conscious. She wondered if she had a mess on her face and that was why the girl had gasped. She dragged a fist across her mouth to clean it.

"M-my apologies, miss," Fabienne stuttered. "It's just…" Her voice trailed off.

"A closed mouth don't eat, child," said Aunt Teddy. "What's on your mind? Why you lookin' at my niece like she a ghost or somethin'?"

"I believe I know her, ma'am." Fabienne looked to Pee Wee. "You got any kin around here?"

Pee Wee nodded. "Got two sisters: one named Betty and one named Ann. Also got me a half-brother named—"

"Betty? Bettina Jean?" Fabienne's cheeks reddened.

Pee Wee's stomach dropped. "Oh, Lord, don't tell me she upstairs."

"Oh, heavens no. Betty would never work in a place like—" Fabienne caught herself, then looked nervously at Miss Kitty to see if the madam had noticed the minor indiscretion. "Bettina and I was at finishin' school together. We was friends for awhile."

"Whatchu mean, 'for awhile'? You ain't friends no more?"

"It ain't that, miss. It's just, y'know, I haven't seen her since she headed north."

Pee Wee's eyes grew wide. "Headed north? When she head north?"

Aunt Teddy sighed and shook her head.

Fabienne's face turned crimson. "My apologies, miss. I thought you knew. I—"

"When she head up north?" Pee Wee pressed.

"About six months ago, I'd reckon. Went with her boyfriend. Said she was gonna come back and finish up school when she was done with her business up there, but she was in a way when she left, and I haven't heard from her since."

"In a way?" Pee Wee said. "What kind of way?"

Before the conversation could continue, Miss Kitty snapped her fan shut loudly. "Merci, Fabienne. That will be all for now. Please return to the kitchen and see what needs attending to."

Fabienne curtsied and took her leave.

"Wait!" Pee Wee said, but Fabienne exited the room without looking back.

"I'm sorry, my dear," Miss Kitty said to Pee Wee. "But I had to cut your conversation short. Fabienne has work to do before her clients arrive. She's on a very tight schedule."

Pee Wee looked to her aunt with pleading in her eyes.

Aunt Teddy sighed. "Go. I can handle our business with Miss Kitty."

Before Aunt Teddy could change her mind, Pee Wee jumped from her seat and raced toward the exit after Fabienne.

Miss Kitty gasped as Pee Wee flew past her, startled by the sudden break from decorum. "Hattie Mae?" She turned to watch the girl exit the room, then turned back to Aunt Teddy. "Where does that niece of yours think she's going?"

"To talk more with that girl of yours, I s'pose."

"Fabienne? But why?"

"Remember when the levy broke?"

"My dear Theodora, of course I do. Who around these parts doesn't?"

"Well, that's the last time Pee Wee saw her sister Betty. Last time she saw any of her family."

"But that was years ago," Miss Kitty said, frowning sympathetically. She made a *tsk* sound with her tongue. "I can't even imagine."

Aunt Teddy knew Miss Kitty was "puttin' on airs," but that was to be expected when dealing with a woman like her. A cost of doing business, some would say. "But back to the matter at hand," Aunt Teddy said. "Who am I seein' today?"

IN THE KITCHEN, Pee Wee jumped around like a cat on a hot griddle, asking Fabienne so many questions and talking so fast that the poor girl finally had to raise her hands up in defeat and beg Pee Wee to slow down.

"I only got two ears," she said while weaving in and out of the many women and girls who were working the kitchen. A group of small children hid beneath one of the preparation tables and giggled as they ate fresh muffins and watched the frenzied workers.

Pee Wee noticed that Fabienne talked differently back here. "Hey, what happened to that fancy accent of yours?"

"That's for company. It's one of the things we learn at finishin' school—how to speak all proper-like. But this is who I really am. I'm from the swamp, just like you."

"Were you *good* friends with my sister?"

Fabienne shrugged. "I s'pose. But no one mattered to your sister as much as that boyfriend of hers. Lord, that boy followed her everywhere. Some days, he would stand outside the schoolyard fence for hours, just waitin' for her to stop by. That was the only contact they had for awhile, until she started sneakin' out with him at night and comin' back early in the mornin' before anyone would notice." Fabienne gave Pee Wee a sly smile. "We all knew what they was up to, just couldn't prove it. Until she told us, that is."

"Told you what?"

"That she was headin' up north to have her baby. That night, she packed up all her stuff and left, didn't come back in the mornin'."

The word "baby" smacked Pee Wee like an iron skillet. *Betty was a mama now?*

Pee Wee could barely get the words out: "She was pregnant?"

"Yeah. But listen, if you wanna keep talkin', you'll have to come on upstairs with me. I gotta get dressed."

"Ain't you dressed already?"

Fabienne chuckled, then grabbed Pee Wee's hand and pulled her toward a set of stairs at the back of the kitchen.

Fabienne had really soft hands, which was surprising to Pee Wee since she assumed all working-class folks had hard hands like hers.

These must be the hands of someone who pours tea and makes desserts for a living, she reasoned.

"Why yo' hands so soft?" Pee Wee asked once they had reached the top of the stairs.

"No man wants to be touched by a woman with hard hands, Pee Wee. Why you *ain't* got soft hands?"

"Cuz I work for a livin'."

Fabienne stopped as if to say something, but thought better of it and continued on down the hall in silence.

The hall was long and dimly lit by candelabras. There were many heavy wooden doors on both sides. A ratty red carpet ran the length of the floor, and shadows danced on an aging floral wallpaper that was starting to peel at the edges. Outside every door was a small table, upon which rested a pitcher of water and a bowl. Scarves had been tied around some of the doorknobs, but not all.

Before Pee Wee could ask about the scarves, Fabienne snatched her into a room at the end of the hall.

"This here's my room. I share it with three other girls, but they's not here right now."

A large bed took up most of the small room, and clothes were strewn everywhere. Beside the bed was a small vanity, a mirror, and a dozen bottles of half-used perfume—the same perfumes that Aunt Teddy sold.

Fabienne picked up the clothes and started shoving them into a nearby dresser as she rambled on and on about Betty, the finishing school, even the life she led before meeting Pee Wee's sister. Pee Wee didn't care much for this part, but since she couldn't get a word in edge-wise, she listened. Listened to Fabienne talk about her life, her childhood, and her parents—how she didn't know her father (a white man, according to her mother) and how her mother worked for Miss Kitty for many years before gifting Fabienne to Miss Kitty as her replacement.

"Mama paid good money for me to go to that school so that I could make somethin' better for myself, but guess what? Here I am anyway. On my back, just like her. Only difference is I ain't ever gonna leave. Miss Kitty treats me real nice, and she lets me see fewer clients than the other girls since I earn more than them per visit. The old white men that frequent this place love to pay whatever it takes to touch me. That means I get to set my own price. " She leaned in close to Pee Wee and whispered, "Sometimes them men give me extra for myself, but don't tell Miss Kitty."

Fabienne whirled around and played with her hair while facing the vanity mirror. The tone in her voice was lighter now. "Is you a conjure woman like your aunt, cuz I really need somethin' to keep me from gettin' pregnant. I only have two clients today, but I can't be takin' any chances. One of them is a preacher."

"But my sister—"

"Betty? What about her?"

"Did she say where up north she was headin'?"

Fabienne continued to look at herself in the mirror, batted her eyes at her reflection. "No. But y'know what? I think her baby is gonna be so pretty. The daddy is so cute. She told us that she was goin' up north to raise her baby right, but never mentioned where exactly. I'm really hopin' nothin' bad happens to her. She promised she was gonna bring the baby back down here when she could. Said I could watch it while she finish school."

Then without warning, Fabienne undressed herself right there in front of Pee Wee until she was standing completely naked.

Pee Wee was shocked at the way Fabienne showed her nude body without any shame. Even a confident woman like Aunt Teddy closed the door when changing clothes. But here was Fabienne, naked in all God's glory, wiping her body down with a wet towel and putting on perfume in front of a stranger.

A part of Pee Wee wanted to peek at Fabienne's body, but the rest of her urged itself backward toward the door, where she slipped out into the hallway without Fabienne noticing. But when Pee Wee turned to head back toward the stairs, she bumped into Alex, who was carrying a basket of fresh linens.

He saw the uncomfortable look on Pee Wee's face and chuckled. "She don't stop once she start, does she?" he said, gesturing to Fabienne's door. He then gave the door a gentle knock.

Fabienne answered the door, now dressed in fresh clothes. "There you are!" she said to Pee Wee. Her voice was soft and as light as a summer breeze. "Come back in! I have questions." Fabienne reached out and grabbed Pee Wee's arm, but Alex stopped her in the doorway.

"Miss Kitty wants her downstairs with Miss Teddy," he said. "They got work to do, Fabienne. 'Sides, so do you. The preacher is on his way now." He handed Fabienne her share of fresh linens, then turned to wink at Pee Wee. "Get away while ya can," he whispered.

And so Pee Wee did.

UPON RETURNING TO the parlor, Aunt Teddy instructed Pee Wee to grab the half-empty box of whiskey bottles and, much to the girl's dismay, follow her back upstairs. Aunt Teddy carried the box of perfumes. The brown bottles in the box jingled and played a light song to Pee Wee's ears as she followed her aunt upstairs.

It was the same hallway as before, but this time, all the women stood in their doors to greet Aunt Teddy. They smiled and waved and asked Aunt Teddy a million questions about men and love.

Pee Wee thought it strange to see Aunt Teddy treated with such reverence. Most folks in town gave her aunt a side eye and a wide berth.

"Do you have that perfume you promised me?" one woman asked. "The one that would make him love only me?"

Aunt Teddy smiled and nodded toward Pee Wee. "Collect for me, would ya?"

Pee Wee took payment from this woman, and all the rest, in the form of paper bills and coins. Some had already laid their money on the floor for easy collection. At the end of the hallway, near Fabienne's room, Aunt Teddy had a little room of her own. She unlocked the door with her key and went inside.

The room was slightly bigger than a closet. Facing the backyard was a huge window through which the sun shone, casting sunbeams over the cracked wood floor. There was no bed in this room, only a small desk and a table. Aunt Teddy placed her box of perfumes on the table in front of the window and took her seat at the desk. Pee Wee placed the half-empty box of whiskey bottles on the table next to the perfumes.

A knock came at the door. Standing in the open doorframe was a rail-thin girl with skin as dark as night and smooth as polished stone.

"Zephra, come in," Aunt Teddy said to the girl. "Don't be shy."

"I'll wait outside," Pee Wee said as Zephra slipped past her into the room. Back in the hallway, she closed the door behind her. That's when she saw Alex approach.

"Pee Wee," he said with a wave. "Want to get lunch with me later? I got chores right now—I gotta run to the store for some stuff for Miss Kitty—but we can go when I get back. What do ya say?"

"Sure, I guess. I also got some work to do, but people gotta eat at some point. Even Aunt Teddy gets hungry, so I'm certain she'll say yes." Pee Wee smiled, thinking nothing of Alex's intentions.

I eat lunch with Bump and the folks at work all the time. This ain't no different. Maybe he'll slip me some of that car'mel cake I saw downstairs. Everythin' in that kitchen looked so sweet and delicious and—

"No, Pee Wee. I mean just you and me. Do you want to have lunch with just me? Your aunt will be busy for awhile, I reckon."

Pee Wee's thoughts paused. She looked at Alex and then at the floor. Her cheeks grew flushed as she grinned. But before she could answer, a woman burst from the stairs and ran down the hall to grab Pee Wee.

She had white-blonde hair that was held back with a big red bow, and she wore a white dress-slip with no shoes. She was out of breath upon her arrival, her white cheeks flushed pink. "You with the conjure woman?" she asked.

"I *am* a conjure woman," Pee Wee replied.

"Good, because we got us a little problem out back." The woman half-dragged Pee Wee down the hallway, with Alex following close behind.

"What is it, Emma?" he asked.

"Nothin' you need to worry about. Just go to the store for Miss Kitty, all right. Fetch her the things she needs. This conjure woman here will help us."

Pee Wee beamed with pride. *This is what it's goin' to be like when I take over for Aunt Teddy,* she thought. *Folks comin' from far and wide in search of me, Pee Wee, the greatest conjure woman alive! I'll never have to leave the house since all the business will come to my doorstep.*

Emma led Pee Wee briskly through the kitchen.

"Where you girls runnin' off to?" a woman hollered from behind a stove.

"It's Betsy!" Emma hollered back. "She needs help!" She pulled Pee Wee out the back door and across the yard to a smaller house hidden behind some trees.

When they reached the small house, Pee Wee heard screams coming from inside, but before she could ask what was going on, Emma pulled her inside and up a narrow flight of stairs. The screams grew louder as they ascended.

When they reached the room where all the noise was coming from, Emma pushed the door open and announced to all inside, "I got us a conjure woman!"

Inside the room were four girls, all a bit older than Pee Wee, standing around a bed and attending to the young girl laying there, who was sweating profusely and in great pain. Blood stained the floor. The girl in the bed grunted, then screamed—the same scream Pee Wee heard on approach. One of the attending girls then pulled back the bed sheet that had been covering the screaming girl to reveal to Pee Wee the cause for all their concern.

Pee Wee's eyes widened at the sight. This wasn't the kind of conjure work she was used to. Love spells? No problem. Making good luck? No problem. But between this girl's legs was something she'd never seen before: a black bubble getting bigger and smaller as the girl on the bed screamed. When she screamed, she squeezed her eyes shut and tensed her muscles, and the bubble grew larger. When she rested, the bubble receded back inside her.

"Bless your heart," Pee Wee said. "You got a baby comin' outta ya."

And then she fainted.

"THE DEAD SHALL rise again," Aunt Teddy proclaimed, laughing as Pee Wee opened her eyes to stare up at the beamed ceiling. Pee Wee turned her head to see her aunt sitting at the tiny desk from before.

Pee Wee scratched at her head. "Where...?"

"You fainted, Pee Wee. I thought you knew all about where babies come from? We had that talk already, didn't we?" Aunt Teddy walked over and shook a glass of ice water in Pee Wee's face. "Drink up. We ain't done yet."

Pee Wee sat up. "'Course I know where babies come from! But that didn't look like no baby I've ever seen. And nobody done told me how messy birthin' was—all that blood and piss everywhere. I thought they was killin' roosters up there in that room. Honest to God."

Aunt Teddy's eyes narrowed. "Enough with that kinda talk. Y'know better than to speak of Voodoo in front of me. When we together, you practice Hoodoo. You hear? If'n you wanna talk about killin' roosters and such, go do it somewhere else."

Pee Wee chugged down the ice water before answering, "Yes'm."

Aunt Teddy set one bottle of whiskey onto the table and an empty bottle beside it. "Good. Cuz you about to be makin' love potions, and I don't need no Voodoo magic messin' up my business. A girl will be showin' up here soon with a special concoction. I want you to take that concoction and put a few drops of what's inside into this here empty bottle. When that's done, add a pour of whiskey and mix it up good. And don't forget to take the girl's money before givin' her whatchu make. Think you can do all that without faintin' this time?"

Pee Wee straightened herself up. "What fool can't do that, Aunt Teddy? I got it."

Aunt Teddy retrieved two items from her conjure bag: a cotton plant and…

"Is that turpentine?" Pee Wee asked. "Whatchu need that for?"

"I'll tell ya later," Aunt Teddy said. She took the cotton plant and turpentine and got up to leave.

"Where you goin'?"

"There's another pregnant girl in this house that needs my help."

Pee Wee looked again at the turpentine. "Oh," she whispered.

Aunt Teddy left the room and closed the door behind her.

Alone now, Pee Wee climbed to her feet and took a seat in the desk chair. She wriggled her butt around on the pillow Aunt Teddy sat on to get comfortable, then started digging around the box of bottles at her feet. She grabbed a cork and a funnel, and set them on the desk. With the tools laid out before her, she started feeling powerful again, and she let the feeling wash over her. A knock came at the door, and she called out to invite her guest in.

A young girl slipped inside and took a seat in the chair across from Pee Wee. She was mixed-race, with loose black curls and honey-colored skin. She wore a white lace ribbon tied around her neck and a cream-colored dress. Black eyeliner framed her green eyes, and they seemed to sparkle against her skin.

"You here for the love potion?" Pee Wee asked.

The girl nodded.

"My aunt says you have somethin' for me. Did you bring it?"

The girl reached down into her exposed cleavage and retrieved a small, thin vial no bigger than a girl's finger. She handed it to Pee Wee. It was still warm from the time spent between her breasts and smelled of sweet-scented soap and fresh-cut flowers.

Pee Wee shook the vial to make the liquid bubble up, then popped the cork with her thumb.

The girl leaned forward and whispered, "It's real fresh."

"Is that so," Pee Wee said, puzzled by the wafting scent. She placed the funnel into the rim of the empty bottle and poured a few measured drops inside. While re-corking the vial, a single drop fell onto the desk and stained the wood red. She handed the vial back to the girl.

"How much do I owe?" the girl asked.

Before she could answer, a devilish little thought occurred to Pee Wee, and she grinned with impish delight. She remembered Fabienne's little trick of setting her own prices and keeping the extra. "Usually, I would mix this with rum," she lied, "but all we got right now is my Aunt Teddy's homemade whiskey. It's real good whiskey, but real expensive too, which means it's gonna cost ya more."

"That's fine," the girl said. "I brought extra." She placed more than enough money onto the desk.

Pee Wee counted the bills with a twinkle in her eye. "That should do it," she said, then poured enough whiskey into the funnel to fill the empty bottle up. "You can make a fine mint julep with this here mixture," Pee Wee said. She set the drained bottle of whiskey down, removed the funnel from the mixture, and shook the bottle up with her thumb covering the opening. She corked the bottle and handed it to the girl.

"I don't know how to make a mint julep," the girl said. "That's the boys' job. They bring them up to our rooms upon request." She held up the bottle that Pee Wee gave her. "I add this in later. Y'know, for love." The girl thanked Pee Wee and then scampered out of the room.

"No money back if it don't work!" Pee Wee yelled.

Pee Wee spent the next hour or so making expensive love potions for one girl after another. By the time Aunt Teddy returned, the money bag on the desk looked about ready to burst.

"Looks like we made a small fortune today," Aunt Teddy said with a smile. She looked beneath the desk to see that the box of whiskey was almost empty of brown bottles.

"Excellent work there, Miss Hattie Mae. You may earn your keep yet."

A light tap interrupted their conversation, and Fabienne entered the room.

"My apologies, Miss Theodora, but I heard you was making love potions. Am I too late?"

"No, ma'am," said Pee Wee. "Come right this way."

"Well, I must apologize first. See, I don't have any blood, so I was wonderin' if there was somethin' else you could give me. Like a love potion made from one of your powders or somethin'? I can pay whatever you want. I got the money."

Pee Wee shook her head. "I'm sorry, what? Whatchu mean, 'blood'?"

Fabienne ringed her hands nervously. "Um…the first drops of my menses. Miss Theodora sent word to us girls to bottle some for your arrival today, but mine hasn't come yet this month, so…"

Pee Wee's stomach dropped. She looked down at the red stain on the desk and then at the reddish-brown stain on her thumb that had come from shaking up all the love potions.

In was then, in that most untimely moment, that Alex popped into the room with news. "Hey, Pee Wee. Since it's such fine weather today, I set us up real nice outside for lunch. Are you ready for a picnic?"

Aunt Teddy covered her mouth so as to stop herself from laughing.

Pee Wee looked to her aunt, then to Fabienne, then to her thumb again, before running over to what she thought was an open window, slamming headfirst into the glass, and vomiting all over the table and floor. After emptying her stomach of its contents, she fell to her knees and motioned to wipe the vomit from her lips, but when she saw even more bloodstains on her fingertips, she screamed out in disgust and fainted.

"She ain't got no kinda constitution, do she?" said Alex.

PEE WEE SAT beside Alex on a checkered blanket in the grass and stretched her arms out wide, the sunshine reflecting off the sparkly dress that Fabienne had lent her. Pee Wee's vomit-stained dress, meanwhile, was drying on a nearby clothesline. Pee Wee listened quietly to a breeze that blew through the trees and enjoyed the fresh scent of magnolias, carried by the winds. She was barefoot now, and her hair was in a single plait, fastened to her head.

"Do you wanna try some berries or somethin'?" Alex asked. "The girls in the kitchen also sent you out some crackers if'n that sounds better for your stomach." Alex handed Pee Wee a glass of fresh-squeezed lemonade.

"Got any biscuits?" Pee Wee asked, taking the drink. She ran her fingers through the cool grass next to the blanket to help relax.

"Yeah. I got a few right here."

Pee Wee studied Alex as he prepared a small plate of biscuits and fruit for her. His hands moved in such a delicate manner, his fingers slender like a woman's. His perfect teeth sparkled in the sun. She sipped her lemonade and smiled at him. "Thanks," she said. She took the plate, and a spark shot through her during the brief moment their fingers touched.

"So, what's it like bein' a conjure woman?" he asked.

Pee Wee shrugged. "Right now I'm just helpin' my aunt, learnin' as much as I can. I'm gonna be the greatest conjure woman ever, y'know."

"Gonna have to get better with blood first, I reckon."

Pee Wee groaned. "I ain't ever felt this sick in my life. My mama always told me never to visit a place like this, but did I listen? No." Pee Wee took a bite from one of the biscuits and was immediately surprised by the sweet taste. She raised an eyebrow. "I never had no *sweet* biscuits before."

Alex laughed. "You like it?"

"Uh-huh."

"Why don't your mama like this place?"

Pee Wee swallowed her bite of biscuit and washed it down with some lemonade. "She say the devil run through the women here. Ain't no redemption for 'em."

"What do you think?"

"Don't know, really. Today I seen a girl have a baby and love it a whole lot, so there's gotta be a little bit of good, at least."

"What about me? Am I good?"

Pee Wee cleared her throat. "Mind passin' me another biscuit, please? They *real* good."

Alex plucked another biscuit from the spread and put it on Pee Wee's plate. He leaned in real close to her and whispered, "What about the devil, Pee Wee? You think the devil is in this place? Think he's sittin' right in front of you now?"

No boy had ever been so close to Pee Wee as Alex was now. She could smell everything that he'd eaten for breakfast that morning.

Meanwhile, her own mouth had gone dry and the biscuit wasn't helping any. Her skin felt hot as a single bead of sweat dripped down her back between her shoulder blades.

"I think that sick is comin' back, Alex," she whispered. "You may wanna move back a bit."

But Alex didn't move. He just flicked his tongue out and licked a biscuit crumb from her lip.

Pee Wee jerked, which caused her to drop her glass of lemonade into the grass. Was she holding her breath? And why was her face so hot all of a sudden? That bead of sweat on her back was now several beads, and she was starting to sweat all over.

"You…*guh*…" Pee Wee stammered. Words escaped her.

"Let me get it," Alex said of the spilled drink. He then leaned across Pee Wee's body to retrieve the fallen glass.

He was freshly bathed, and his neck smelled like soap, and Pee Wee felt her body struggling to decide between running far away or grabbing the boy and holding him extra tight. No boy ever made her feel like this. She willed herself not to faint again as Alex placed a hand on the small of her back.

"You okay, Pee Wee?"

"Lord, have mercy—" Pee Wee gasped. She could see now that his green eyes had brown flecks in them, could hear the clicking of his tongue when he slyly smiled.

"You really look purtier than a peach in that dress," he told her. "Maybe you should consider—"

But before he could finish the thought, Pee Wee reached up and slapped him hard across the face. "How dare you insult me like that!"

Alex rubbed the spot on his cheek where Pee Wee had struck him. "Good Lord, Pee Wee. I was only gonna say that you should ask Fabienne if'n you could keep that dress, since it looks so good on you. You didn't have to go and slap me."

Pee Wee looked down at the shimmering dress. It was a sheer white chiffon, adorned by a brocade of lace and pearls. "I'm sorry. I thought you was implyin' somethin'—that I was a loose woman, which I am not."

"I never thought ya were." He gathered up the food and plates.

"I'm sorry, Alex. Really, I am."

Alex looked over at her. "Well, it might feel better if'n ya kissed it. Just a lil kiss, is all."

A warmth surged through Pee Wee, and without thinking much about it, she leaned in and planted a small kiss on Alex's cheek, where her hand print had started to blossom red.

From behind them, Aunt Teddy loudly cleared her throat. "I can't leave you alone for a minute, can I?"

Pee Wee pulled back from Alex and blushed something terrible.

IT WAS A little after lunch when Lone Wolf pulled back up with the wagon. Pee Wee was sitting on the porch with Alex, and Aunt Teddy was inside talking to the girls about protecting themselves.

"No offense, but I really don't want to come back to this place," Pee Wee said to Alex. She was wearing her own dress again, and it felt so much heavier and less classy than the dress that Fabienne had lent her, but fortunately for Pee Wee, Fabienne saw her in the borrowed dress and let her keep it since she liked how good it looked on her.

Alex kicked at the dirt and fidgeted with his hands like he didn't know what to do with himself.

From behind them, the front door opened and out came Aunt Teddy, followed closely by Miss Kitty.

"Why, Theodora, I can't thank you enough! You were fantastic today! As they say in France, *Laissez les bon temps roulez!*"

"Can I come see you, sometime?" Alex asked Pee Wee.

The dress Fabienne had gifted Pee Wee was draped over the porch railing, and when Pee Wee stood to leave, she grabbed it. "I didn't wanna draw too much attention, but now that you mention it, I do have this dress, and I'm gonna need to wear it somewhere nice." She winked at Alex and followed her aunt to the wagon.

Aunt Teddy climbed into the seat beside Lone Wolf, and Pee Wee climbed into the back with the empty boxes.

Pee Wee faced out the back of the wagon as they departed and watched Alex wave goodbye to her from the porch.

She smiled and waved back.

"See ya soon, I hope," she said quietly to herself.

PEE WEE THROWS THEM BONES

"Power tends to corrupt, and absolute power corrupts absolutely."

—Lord Acton

IN LOUISIANA, FALL arrives later than it does in the states up north, but when it does arrive, it brings the one thing everyone in Pee Wee's parish had been waiting for all summer long: cooler weather. The lower temperatures of fall meant folks didn't sweat so much, and that was a good thing, especially for Pee Wee, who spent every summer sweating her pressed head of hair out. Straight one minute, curly the next. During those hottest months, she thought often about just chopping all her thick locks off, but never made good on the idea because she was too afraid of looking like a boy with short hair.

She thought about that as she kicked at the dead leaves on the ground on her way home from her job at the butcher shop. The crisp fall air felt good, and she was barely sweating at all, even after hours of handling heavy cuts of meat. She was tired, but the stroll had been a pleasant one so far, so she really had no reason to complain.

Winds whispered and bees buzzed. The strong scents of honeysuckle, moss, and freshly plowed earth filled her nose.

Upon arriving back at Aunt Teddy's house, Pee Wee trudged up the back steps and went straight to her bedroom, where she peeled off her heavy work-apron—stained red from all the animal blood—and tossed it carelessly onto the floor. The house smelled like baked apples, which meant Aunt Teddy was baking another delicious apple pie.

Normally, Pee Wee would head to the kitchen to check on the pie, but not today. Instead, she felt the sudden urge to search her room for something very specific and small. After flipping enough pillows and moving enough sheets, she finally found what she was looking for and made a little gasping noise when she did. It was an old handkerchief that belonged to her mother. Why she wanted it just now, she didn't know, but she knew what she planned to do with it. With handkerchief in hand, she retrieved some black thread and a sewing needle from her dresser, then took her wares to the enclosed porch and sat on the floral-cushioned couch.

Once settled, she carefully threaded the needle and used it to sew a large black circle in the center of the handkerchief. Again, Pee Wee wasn't certain why she felt the need to do this. She just *did*. Almost as if she was being compelled by someone or something beyond her control.

That's when a thought occurred to her.

"Viola?" she whispered. "You there?"

No response. Just silence.

Pee Wee closed her eyes and focused hard on Viola's name, but still nothing. When she heard Aunt Teddy coming, she opened her eyes and cleared her throat.

Aunt Teddy, her belly swollen with child, wandered out to the porch with a bowlful of blueberries, and heaved her weight onto the sofa next to Pee Wee. "Whatchu doin'?" she asked. She popped a few blueberries into her mouth.

Pee Wee shrugged. "Nothin' really. Somethin' told me to start sewin', so here I am, doin' just that. I've been makin' it a point to listen closely to the spirits, so as I don't piss them off again." Pee Wee tilted her head to the side and studied the black circle she stitched into the cloth.

Aunt Teddy ate another blueberry. "Y'know, you should really start gettin' your bone set together. I did a throw the other day, and I think you gonna be leavin' us soon."

Pee Wee snapped her head toward Aunt Teddy. "Whatchu mean, *leavin'*? I ain't goin' nowhere 'til you have that baby. I wanna see what a half-Injun baby look like. I think with all that burpin' you doin', that baby gonna come out with a head full of hair, and it's gonna be one long plait down the back."

"Born with a plait? Pee Wee, you crazy." Aunt Teddy snickered.

Pee Wee made a small sound and went back to her sewing. But then something small hit her in the face… And another something… And another, until she realized Aunt Teddy was throwing blueberries at her. Pee Wee sat up and shook her finger at her aunt. "Don't go throwin' good food at me! We got no money to waste!"

"I see you learnin', huh?" Aunt Teddy laughed, then grunted. She pointed at her belly, covered with a thin white shirt, and Pee Wee watched it move.

"She agree with me." Pee Wee laughed.

"Maybe it's a he," said Lone Wolf. He strolled out of the house with his dirty farming clothes on, and joined them on the porch.

"Well, *he's* gonna be born with one long plait," Pee Wee mumbled.

Lone Wolf reached down and patted Teddy's belly, then sat at her feet and rubbed some kind of salve on her ankles. Stuff smelled like peppermint.

"I was just tellin' Hattie Mae here that she should start gatherin' herself a bone throwin' bag," Aunt Teddy said to Lone Wolf. "She gon' be leavin' us soon."

"I don't even know what a bone throwin' bag is," said Pee Wee. "And stop tellin' people I'm leavin'!"

Aunt Teddy pulled a small bag from her pocket. "Hold out yo' hand," she told Pee Wee. Then she dumped the contents of the bag into her niece's waiting hands. It was just a handful of trinkets: a small bell, some marbles, a few acorns, and a couple of keys.

"Why you just pour a buncha junk in my hand?" Pee Wee asked.

"It ain't junk, Hattie Mae. They's my bones. They's how I see the future."

"How's a marble help you see the future?"

"That's the secret: I decide. I use them marbles to predict if there's somethin' good or bad comin'. If'n I throw them and they stay close, that means stay close to your family cuz some bad news is comin'. If'n they spread out, that means you gonna be on your own, but good news is comin' and maybe it's somethin' that only you should hear."

"That don't make no kinda sense."

"You'll see. Just get yourself some bones. We'll talk 'bout the rest later."

Lone Wolf nudged Aunt Teddy, which made her take something from his hair and add it to Pee Wee's hand.

Pee Wee stared at the small iridescent shell.

"It was given to me a long time ago," said Lone Wolf. "And now I'm giving it to you."

"What's it do?"

"Tells you the truth."

"Truth, huh?" Pee Wee looked at the stuff in her hand.

"No ticklin'!" Aunt Teddy blurted, kicking Lone Wolf's hands away from her toes.

The two of them shared a playful laugh until they were interrupted by the sound of someone banging on the back door downstairs.

"I'll go see who it is," said Pee Wee. She set Aunt Teddy's trinkets in her ma's handkerchief, wrapped it up so they wouldn't fall out, and shoved it in her pants pocket. She then ran through the house and down the stairs to answer the door.

Outside stood Etienne, a boy from the settlement down the way. He was a "tall glass of water," as Teddy would say, but Pee Wee called him Tiny on account of his name. According to her, it was too much work to pronounce, and he didn't deserve the effort.

"Whatchu want, Tiny?" she asked. She put her hand on her hip and blocked the entrance into the house.

Hunched over and looking down at Pee Wee, Tiny squinted at her with his green catlike eyes. He was an odd one. A freckle-faced, curly haired beanpole with terrible posture and clothes that always looked two sizes too small or four sizes too big. The blocky black shoes on his feet looked heavy and uncomfortable. "Is your aunt around?" he asked.

"She upstairs. Whatchu need?"

"I need another castin'. I got questions that only Teddy can answer." He tried to look beyond Pee Wee, but what she lacked in height, she made up for in stature.

"Y'know what to do," Pee Wee said, pointing to an empty bucket on the floor.

Tiny opened his mouth to protest, but Pee Wee stopped him with an "Uh-uh! No!" and pointed at the bucket again. She tapped it with her toe for emphasis.

Tiny grumbled while rooting around in his pocket for payment, but even after he dropped a few coins into the bucket, Pee Wee stopped him from pushing past her.

"Add to it," she said.

"That's all I got," he pleaded, trying again to look over her head and into the house.

"I know you got some dollars. I seen you back in the alley on Grove, gamblin' with Bump. You two is always playin' dice and whatnot, and you's always the one winnin'." She crossed her arms and pointed down at the bucket again.

Tiny dropped a few pieces of paper money in the bucket. "Fine! Happy now?"

"Whatchu need, Tiny?" Pee Wee pressed.

"Teddy! I need Teddy!" He shouted into the house for Aunt Teddy until Pee Wee finally let him pass.

She stepped aside and hollered up the stairs after him. "Aunt Teddy! Tiny's here for you!"

Once Tiny was out of sight, she scooped the paper money from the bucket and hid it inside her sock. Then she followed the boy upstairs.

PEE WEE WAS hiding in the living room and eaves-droppping on Tiny and Aunt Teddy's conversation on the porch when Lone Wolf told the pair he would give them their privacy and headed into the living room as well, expecting to be alone. But when he turned the corner to see Pee Wee holding a finger to her lips to shush him, he smiled and joined her in eavesdropping.

"I ain't know you was bad like me, Mista Wolf," Pee Wee whispered, grinning.

He chuckled and moved his ear closer to the doorway so he could hear better.

"Miss Teddy, please," Tiny pleaded. "I just need one more throw. I done paid Pee Wee already and ev'rythin'. Throw again or give me somethin' for luck, at least! If'n I come home with no money, my ma is gonna beat me."

Aunt Teddy took a moment before responding. "I got one more thing to give ya, but I'm not doin' no more throwin'. You don't listen, and you screw up ev'rythin', boy! Y'know, I had a vision of you the other night, and I didn't like it. You was hangin' from a tree, neck broke. Now, tell me, who you done crossed?"

"Well, see…" Tiny stumbled over his words until Aunt Teddy stopped him.

"How you gonna stand there and lie to me? Don't you know who you talkin' to? I can read yo' face like a book!"

"Sorry, Miss Teddy!" Tiny said. "I'm sorry!"

"Boy, give me somethin' so I can hit you with it! Stay here!"

Pee Wee and Lone Wolf scampered toward the kitchen upon hearing Aunt Teddy rise from the sofa and head their way. But when Aunt Teddy's hand nearly slipped from the doorjamb while using it to turn the corner into the living room, Lone Wolf changed plans and ran back over to assist her. He tried to help her walk comfortably, but she just swatted him away. She made her way to a chest of drawers and dug through one of the drawers until she finally found what she was looking for—a small red pouch—and palmed it. She called Tiny into the living room.

Tiny stumbled as he ran into the room and skidded to a stop in front of Aunt Teddy.

She handed him the red pouch. "This here is my last piece of good luck. I need you to take it and get outta here. Don't come back. When you ready to throw them dice, put this in yo' mouth. I ain't wastin' my High John the Conquerer on you again." Teddy pressed the small bag into his hand and closed his fingers around it with enough force to nearly break them.

"I appreciate it, Miss Teddy. When I win, I'll bring you mo' money!" Tiny's face went from being absent of color to being filled with it. His cheeks flushed red, and his entire body relaxed. "You never let me down, Miss Teddy!"

"Heed what I say and watch who you gamble with!" she said to Tiny, but the boy was already rushin' down the stairs without listening.

Aunt Teddy shook her head and walked into her bedroom. Pee Wee followed.

"You okay,?" Pee Wee asked.

Aunt Teddy sat on the edge of the bed and gently rubbed her belly. "No one listens to me," she said to her stomach. "But you gonna listen to me, won't ya? Me and yo' Aunt Pee Wee."

Pee Wee's face lit up, and she ran over to Aunt Teddy. She put her nose on the woman's belly and kissed it. "Yep, listen to yo' aunt Pee Wee! I'm a take good care of ya!"

"I hope so." Aunt Teddy exhaled. "She gonna need it."

Pee Wee kissed her aunt's belly again, then got up to leave.

"Where you goin'?"

"Gonna go look for some bones for my bone kit. But don't worry none. I'll be back by supper."

Aunt Teddy laid down on her bed and closed her eyes to rest. "All right, then. Just don't go gettin' into any trouble, ya hear?"

But no response came. Pee Wee had already left.

TINY WAS STILL loitering outside the house when Pee Wee appeared with her conjure bag and bone kit. When he saw her, his face lit up. "Have you come to help me, Pee Wee?" He bounced around her like a dog that was smelling fresh food in her pockets.

"What're you still doin' here, Tiny? Don't you have mo' money to lose?"

Tiny pointed at the bone kit in her hand. "You come to throw bones for me?"

Pee Wee furrowed her brow, annoyed. "You know I can't throw bones, Tiny. I don't know how. But even if I did, I wouldn't waste a throw on you."

Tiny stopped bouncing. "Okay. But what if I give you part of what I win?"

"What if I gave ev'rybody in Hell ice water? No! Now git! I know the trouble you in, and I don't want nothin' to do with it. I may be reckless, but I ain't stupid."

Tiny dropped to his knees in front of her and clasped his hands in prayer. Pee Wee opened her mouth to dress him down, but she saw a vision of him being chased by a group of men. They were angry and shaking their hands at him, yelling things out about him, that he was a cheater and a thief. Someone had a rope and tossed it around his neck. Then she saw him swinging from a tree, kicking his legs and struggling until the life was drained from him.

The men gathered beneath him and started taking his shoes and socks. Someone cut off his pants and another took his shirt. They left Tiny hanging in the tree, naked as the day he was born. The attackers disappeared and the sky turned to night. Flames erupted from unseen torches all around her, and their violent flickering cast her shadow across the boy's hanging body, the rope making a terrible creaking sound in the branches above as his body swung back and forth with the wind. She reached out to touch him. His feet were cold like ice. That's when a hand touched her shoulder.

"Leave him be, child," said the owner of the hand. "Nothin' you can do." He was a Black man in a suit and hat.

Pee Wee tried to speak, but she couldn't. The rope was around her neck now. But before she could panic, the man touched the rope, and it disappeared.

"Now, go," he said. His smile was bright, like a million stars shining in her eyes. But when she blinked, the vision was no more. She stared down at the still-kneeling Tiny. "Where you go gamblin'?" she asked.

The boy looked up from his clasped hands, confused. "Huh? I don't understand."

"I saw somethin' just now, and it wasn't good. I think Aunt Teddy was right. If'n you go wherever you plannin' to go, you gonna die."

Tiny's eyes grew wide like saucers. "You saw it, too?"

"I may not like you much, Tiny, but I want you to live a good, long life so you can see me become the best conjure woman ever. But if'n you go gamblin', you ain't gonna see tomorrow. I think you done crossed somebody dangerous, Tiny. Somebody real dangerous."

Tiny shook the fear from his eyes, then climbed back to his feet. He looked down at her and laughed. "Ain't nothin' gonna happen to me, Pee Wee. Not while I got this black cat bone." He showed Pee Wee the red pouch Aunt Teddy gave him.

Pee Wee crossed her arms, defiant. "Well, just know that when you die—and you gonna—I'm comin' for what's left of you. Gonna dig you up and peel yo' skin back real slow." Pee Wee pretended to peel off her own face at the jawline.

Tiny gasped and took a step back. "But why?"

"So I can take your jawbone. Don't ya read yo' Bible? Samson killed a hundred thousand men with the jawbone of a donkey. And you's a true jackass if'n you gonna do whatchu gonna do. So, I'll have the power of a hundred thousand men and then some."

"I ain't no donkey, Pee Wee!"

"Says you."

Tiny watched in stunned silence as Pee Wee continued on down the path.

"By the way," she said to him, taking a moment to turn back. "Aunt Teddy never did anoint that there black cat bone. It ain't gonna help you none." She paused for a moment, then added, "Just thought you should know that." She smiled and carried on her way.

PEE WEE WHISTLED a tune as she strolled through the forest to her old home. Figuring it a good place to find some bones for her bone kit, she stopped by Viola's house and summoned her.

"Viola, show me where you at," Pee Wee whispered as she stepped across the threshold and into the dark house.

Stray beams of sunlight played on the dust that coated what few belongings remained: a burned chair, some charred scraps of fabric on the floor, an ash-covered desk pushed into the corner, with small boxes on top of it. A veve was drawn on the floor, meant to invoke the spirit of Voodoo god Baron Samedi, loa of the dead. Pee Wee scuffed her feet across it.

"Can't betray my ancestors," she muttered.

It was then that Viola showed her true self to Pee Wee. Gone was the young girl that caught her in the forest. Standing before her now was a stooped old woman with wrinkled brown skin. She wore a white scarf on her head and a white dress that hung loose on her skeletal frame, looking many sizes too big. Viola had one good eye, and the other was a milky white. Some bad men had taken her eye a long time ago, but Viola never told Pee Wee why. When Pee Wee asked why she was still missing her eye in the afterlife, Viola told her that what you look like when you die is what you look like when you're dead. No new body. No new eye.

"Girl, whatchu want?" Viola said.

"I'm buildin' a bone kit. Need to find some stuff for bones. Do you know about throwin' bones?"

"I'm a Voodoo woman, Pee Wee, not stupid. I know more about Hoodoo than you do, and I know all about bone throwin', yes. Now c'mon over this way. I think I got some cowrie shells, but I'm gonna need yo' hands to get 'em."

"You gonna take me over again? Viola, you can't do that without askin' me." Pee Wee crossed her arms. "Last time you did, I was all drunk, and I ain't like it one bit."

A serpentine smile crept across Viola's face. "Yes, I remember. Fun night."

Pee Wee made a disapproving noise.

"But I don't need to be in you this time. I just need for you to come here and fetch it for me. Right here, under the floorboard." Viola pointed down.

Pee Wee did as instructed and walked over to where Viola was pointing. She loosened the floorboard there and found a small purple drawstring bag beneath it. The bag was covered in ash and spiderwebs, but Pee Wee just wiped them away and grabbed the bag, then opened it.

Inside the bag were marbles and colored beads. A few cowrie shells fell out as well. The beads were shiny and looked new.

"I figure you need to have somethin' to show you what's comin'. A cluster of beads mean bad news and spread-out beads mean good news. Everythin' in that bag gonna protect you."

Pee Wee put everything back in the bag and pocketed it. From her conjure bag, she pulled out a piece of char-coal and drew a veve on the loose floorboard. When she finished, she highlighted areas of it with a white piece of chalk. Then she wiped her hands together and stood, marveling at her work.

Viola drifted over. "Who veve is this?"

"This here is *my* veve." Pee Wee stuck her chin out.

"Oh? And who would you be?"

"Pee Wee, Knower of All Things Hoodoo and Voodoo. A strong, Black conjure woman and keeper of spirits."

Viola made a sound that could have been a laugh stuck in her throat. "You? A keeper of spirits?"

"Yes'm. Watch me." Pee Wee pulled a safety pin from her pocket and said, "Viola, I bind you left, I bind you right, I bind you to only be in my sight. I bind you up, I bind you down, I bind you by air, earth, water, and tree. Viola, I bind your spirit to serve only me."

At first, Viola laughed confidently as Pee Wee chanted the spell over and over again, but once Viola's spirit started being stretched thin like a wisp of smoke, she screamed for Pee Wee to stop. But Pee Wee did not stop, and Viola's spirit body was pulled thinner and thinner until it was thin enough to be wound around the safety pin in the girl's hand. Viola howled and scratched at the walls of her tiny prison, trying whatever she could to free herself from Pee Wee's binding, but nothing she tried worked. Pee Wee wrapped the pin again and spoke faster until she finished with, "As I will it so, let it be. This spirit is now in service to me."

With Viola's spirit wound around the safety pin, Pee Wee wrapped a piece of red velvet around the safety pin and tied it tight with a length of black string. She then dropped the bound Voodoo spirit into her conjure bag and smiled.

She walked over to her old house and took a seat on the front porch . She pulled her legs beneath her and placed her conjure bag in front of her, then went through the items inside. She was pulling the smaller bags from the larger bag and organizing them on the porch when she sensed someone nearby and looked up to see Bump.

He walked over and stood in front of her. "Pee Wee, whatchu doin'?"

"Mindin' mine. What about you?"

"I was hopin' for a favor."

Pee Wee looked up at Bump.

"Whatchu need?"

"Teddy told me you was gettin' a bone kit together. Can ya throw for me?" He sat next to her on the porch. She noticed the slight smell of soap, like he'd just bathed, and a hint of sweat, like he was nervous.

She chuckled to herself and faced him. "I don't know what I'm doing yet. I can't throw nothin'. Why you need for me to throw?"

"Well, I did somethin' dumb, and I need some luck."

"Least you is man enough to admit it. What'd you do?"

Bump stared at his hands and cleared his throat. "If'n I tell you, you gotta promise not to be mad. I really need yo' help."

"Whatchu mean, I can't be mad? If this is somethin' stupid, you're on your own."

He sighed like the weight of the world was on his shoulders. He looked at her, smiling broadly, and his eyes sparkled in the sunlight. He took a deep breath, then spoke, "I lost some money—a *lot* of money. I was playin' dice with some of the guys at work and—"

"Y'know how I feel about dice, Bump, considerin' that's how my pa died."

Bump frowned. "You promised not to get mad."

"Did I?" Pee Wee bowed her head and gestured for him to proceed.

"One of them guys told me that since I was winnin', we should try our luck at the races. Next thing I know, we win a few races, and I decided to go for the whole thing—"

Pee Wee sighed. "And you lost."

"And I lost."

"Well, y'all livin' in my house, so you don't need to pay no rent. And if'n you need money for food, I'm sure Aunt Teddy can help you out for a bit. She might wanna whup you for it, but she ain't gonna let you starve."

Bump shook his head. "It gets worse, Pee Wee. See, I also borrowed some money from the guy because he said it was a sure bet. Now Tiny and me—"

"You went to the races with Tiny? That boy is as dumb as the day is long! Git! I changed my mind. I'm not gonna help y'all." Pee Wee gathered up the smaller bags and started angrily placing them back into the larger bag. "Not gonna catch me usin' my Hoodoo to help two knuckleheads get outta trouble," she grumbled to herself.

"Please!" Bump begged. "Do me this one favor and I won't never bother you again. Promise."

"Why should I? What do I get outta this?"

Bump held his head in his hands for a minute before looking Pee Wee directly in the eyes. "I'm beggin' you, Pee Wee. Just this once. Throw them bones and tell me what they say."

Pee Wee saw the pain in Bump's eyes and looked away before he could see the tears forming in hers. "My pa died right here after bein' shot over a gamblin' debt, Bump, and you gonna ask me like this. Really?"

"But that's how you know I'm in trouble. I would never ask you otherwise." He paused, then added, "I'm scared."

Pee Wee wiped the tears from her eyes without Bump seeing and quickly got up before he could stop her. She walked to the front door of the house and took hold of the door handle. "I don't know, Bump. I needs time to think about it." She tried the handle, but it wouldn't budge.

"It's locked, dummy," Bump said, his voice still sad. He got up and walked over to her, placed the key in her hand. "Take some time to think, Pee Wee. I'll be back."

Pee Wee unlocked the door and went inside. She slammed the door behind her and fell against it. "How stupid can he get?"

Pee Wee looked around at the ghosts of her parents—Ma making coffee while Pa walked out the bedroom with his shirt half-buttoned. She could hear Ann and Betty upstairs, snoring along with her past self. Sometimes, Pee Wee would sneak downstairs early and spend time just watching her parents, like she did now. Pee Wee watched her younger self enter the room.

"Well, look who's up!" Pa said. *"Hey lil lady! My Pee Wee! Come sit here with yo' Pa."* Pa's huge hand patted the empty chair next to him.

Ma put a steaming cup of black coffee in front of him and joked with Pee Wee. *"You need some too, ma'am?"*

"No, ma'am. But if'n ya got biscuits and honey, I'd be right pleased."

"Well, yes'm. Biscuits comin' right up."

The aroma of that coffee smelled so good, drifting around the cabin. Ma put the biscuits in the oven and then went outside to get some eggs for Pee Wee's sisters.

"Pa, you like workin' on the railroad?" Pee Wee's past-self asked.

"Not really. It's hard work. Why you askin'?"

"Well, I just hate when you leave. You stay gone for so long."

She watched his hands envelop the dark cup and take a long sip. His eyes shone like dark jewels, and his wavy hair seemed to lay on it's side, like good hair should. Pee Wee smiled at her pa. She really did love him an awful lot.

"Your ma likes it when I come back. She gets money from me to go buy material and sit with Skeet to make quilts. She buys you girls new shoes and stuff for school. It's real important that I go away and work hard. I gotta follow the railroad.

"And besides, we plan on sendin' y'all to finishin' school, or whatever y'all want. Just as long as you don't end up like us—workin' for some man that you never see and hopin' for money that you may or may not get." He rested his hand atop Pee Wee's hand on the table and smiled at her.

"Y'all just want better for us girls?"

He nodded his head and smiled. She liked how Pa's smile was perfect. His skin was so dark that his teeth looked whiter than his white shirt.

Pee Wee closed her eyes to stop herself from crying over the memory. When she opened them again, her pa and younger self were gone. Now she saw her ma standing at the window and staring out. Probably waiting for Pee Wee and her sisters to come walking home from school, or maybe waiting for Pa to come walking down the same trail with money for her, and pralines for the girls.

She smelled her father's cologne wrapping itself around her. It lifted her up and almost twirled her around in the air. It smelled like pine trees and wild bergamot, with a hint of roses. And she knew he was there with her. In the house. Right now.

"Pa, you here?" Pee Wee whispered.

"Pee Wee." She heard his voice and recognized the sound of his steps, walking out of the bedroom. "What are you doin', girl?"

Pee Wee spun around to see him just standing there outside the bedroom door like it was the most normal thing in the world.

"Pa!" Pee Wee cried. She started to run towards him, then stopped. The excitement on her face faded. "You ain't really here, is you?"

"I'm as here as you want me to be." He smiled and opened his arms.

Pee Wee hesitated, then ran over and jumped into his arms, let him wrap himself around her. She cried into his shirt. "Pa, I miss you so much. I do."

"I miss you too, Pee Wee. But right now, your ma needs you more than me. I need for you to go be with her. She's having all kinds of trouble with Patricia Ann. Your sister don't really want to do much around the house to help her cuz she's worried about you and Betty all the time." He released the embrace and walked into the bedroom and sat on the edge of the bed.

Pee Wee stood in the doorway, looking at how his "weight" created an indentation in the bed beneath him.

"She know I'm studying," Pee Wee said. "I get stronger every day, Pa!"

"I come to tell you a few things, Pee Wee. The first is to head to the cemetery and look for a tombstone. A man by the name of Elijah. Died a while ago. You need to break open his coffin and get his jawbone. Then you want to take them iron nails from his coffin."

"What for? He gonna come haunt me or somethin'? I already got enough trouble with these idiot boys out here."

"No, he ain't gonna haunt you. I knew him, but he did some bad things, and that jawbone will be from a hanged man. He was hung for stealing a lot. He always said that if'n he was gonna do it, then he'd do it all the way. Get them nails, too. I'm predictin' you gonna need them soon."

"Okay, Elijah's jawbone and coffin nails," Pee Wee repeated.

"Iron nails. They gonna be a little heavy, but I knows you can do it. My Hattie Mae can do anything. You keep that with yo' kit. Understand?"

Pee Wee nodded.

"When you get real good, I'll come to you again. I'm always watchin' you, Pee Wee. Now go, here comes Bump and some other boy. Watch that other boy. Somethin' ain't right with him. Now go."

"I love you so much, Pa."

Pee Wee wiped the tears from her eyes and turned from the bedroom doorway to see Bump and Tiny enter the house.

"Y'all just can't keep away, huh?" she said.

"Who was you talkin' to?" Bump asked.

"I was mindin' my own. Whatchu want, boy?" Pee Wee put her hand on her hip and jutted it out a bit.

"Have you had enough time to think?" Bump asked. "It's been a few hours now."

A few hours? Pee Wee thought. *Had it really been that long?*

"Bump told me you was thinkin' about throwin' for him," Tiny said. "You wouldn't say no to your own cousin, would ya?"

Pee Wee pointed an accusatory finger at Tiny. "Spirits done told me you ain't right, Tiny. I won't throw with you around. Be gone 'fore I root ya to where you stand." Pee Wee motioned like she was sweeping him away with her hand.

"But…I… C'mon, Pee Wee."

"I'm not in the mood, boy!" Pee Wee stepped forward one step, and Tiny took two steps back. "Now, get outta my house! Bump, you can stay. The spirits want me to help you."

Bump looked at Tiny and nodded at the door, motioning for him to go. Defeated, Tiny hung his head and left.

"Watchu want me to do?" Pee Wee asked Bump.

"You's the conjure woman. Can't you use them bones to predict the dice numbers or somethin'?"

"You want me to help you cheat? You oughta be ashamed."

Bump sniffed the air. "It smells real strange in here. You got a man in here or somethin'?"

"Why? You jealous? When you need to pay back your debts?"

"Tomorrow. But they gonna be throwin' tonight, so I got one more shot at winnin' the money back before I gots real problems. Can you come with? Maybe Hoodoo-up the dice or somethin'."

"First, I can't just 'Hoodoo-up the dice' or somethin'. Don't work like that. Second, cheatin' is wrong and—"

Pee Wee stopped talking as she saw for a second time the vision of Tiny swinging by his neck from a tree.

Pee Wee closed her eyes and felt them roll back in her head. She sighed before she opened them again. "Fine, I'll help you. But you gotta do somethin' for me in return."

"Oh, thank you, Pee Wee! Thank you!" Bump ran over to hug her, but her face said no. She held out her hand for him to shake.

"After we done, I need for you to go to the cemetery with me. I got some errands to run. And Tiny can't come around no more. Spirits don't like him."

Bump nodded his head several times before turning and running out the door.

"I'll meet you at Aunt Teddy's later, and we can go into town together."

THAT NIGHT, BUMP held Pee Wee's hand and half-pulled, half-guided her through the streets to where he and the other boys threw dice. The way the lamps shone on the brick streets made it seem like another world. Hardly anyone was out that night, but as they approached an alley, Pee Wee knew this was the place.

Inside the alley, spirits stood with hats pulled low over their eyes and nodded at her as she was pulled past them. She yanked her hand free from Bump's grip.

"Stop pullin' me! I'm tryin' to listen!"

"Are there spirits here? Whatchu see Pee Wee? What they sayin'?"

"Bump, is you on something? You real jumpy tonight, and I don't think my bones will like that." Pee Wee stepped back and furrowed her brow.

"I'm fine. I'm just ready! Feels like I got me a secret that nobody know about—and that's you, best conjure woman ever!" A trickle of sweat had formed on his brow, and he wiped it away with the back of his hand.

"Best give it a shot right here, sis." Pee Wee heard a voice say.

She looked around and saw an older man wearing a black suit. The one that warned her about Tiny. He leaned against the alley wall, one of his legs straight and the other bent at the knee, with his shoe pressed against the wall.

"Who are you, and why should I listen to you?"

The man ran his fingers along the brow of his hat and lifted his head enough for her to see a smile stretch across his face. "Call me Sam." He exhaled a ring of smoke. "You won't be able throw in there, y'know. They ain't gonna let ya. They don't believe in that Hoodoo like you do." He chuckled and put a toothpick in his mouth.

"If'n that's whatchu say."

Bump shook Pee Wee by the shoulder. "Who you talkin' to? A spirit? What they look like?"

Pee Wee pushed him off her. "Shut up, Bump." She squatted down and pulled the bone kit from her bag. She didn't bring all her bones, just enough to tell her if Bump was gonna have good luck tonight or not.

First, Pee Wee grabbed a piece of black chalk and used it to draw a circle on the ground. Then, she wiped her hands on her black slacks and pulled the bones from her bone kit, one item at a time. "This here is my Pa's black cat bone, chicken bones I found near my house from one of Betty's stews, and these are some pennies from a preacher man's grave."

Bump opened his mouth to say something, but Pee Wee shot a glance at him. Then she looked at the man across the way, who was now leaning forward to see what she was doing. The man chuckled in his throat and picked at his teeth with the toothpick.

There were a few lights shining in the alley, and Pee Wee had a great view of her circle and the stuff from her kit. She held everything in her hands, pulled them close to her, and said a quick prayer. Then she loosed her hands and made the throw.

The spirit man with the toothpick purred as he ran his hand over the spread. He chuckled in his throat. "Not bad. Not bad at all."

Pee Wee studied the bones. Everything was close together. The black cat bone was right next to the stack of chicken bones, and of the six pennies she had, all six landed on heads. Nothing had gone outside the circle. Pee Wee sighed.

"What's it say?" Bump asked.

"It says that no one has any problems with you, and you got some good luck comin' your way. Six heads on a preacher-man penny is really good luck. I'm not gonna throw again."

"Hot damn! I'm headin' in!" Bump ran down the alley before realizing he left Pee Wee. "Pick up your stuff and come on."

Pee Wee focused on grabbing all her bones and putting them back in her kit as she said, "Hey Mista…uh, Sam… should I go with?" But when she looked up, he was gone. He had left his toothpick on the ground, though, and she thought about grabbing it.

"Alright, Bump! I'm coming!"

Bump led Pee Wee to the alley entrance of one of the most lowdown, dirty brothels Pee Wee had ever seen. Women with missing limbs and teeth held the door and passed out drinks. Some of them tried to take Bump to their rooms, to turn a quick profit, but Bump was here for one thing only: to get his money back.

Pee Wee was sure she saw at least one or two men dressed as women, and a lot of women dressed as men. She knew better than to say something, so she followed Bump to a back room on the first floor.

She giggled to herself as she walked by a piano player that sounded like a hound dog singing. To her left was a long bar filled with patrons. To her right and in front of her were the tables. There were several brown doors along the back wall and Bump pushed one open and slid inside the room. But before Pee Wee could follow, she looked over and saw Sam pointing toward a different door. She ran over and opened it, then mumbled thanks as she went inside.

She was greeted by the seedy sight of several men and boys gathered in a circle around a small pile of money on the floor. There was one man that seemed to be the leader, and everyone followed his lead. She saw Bump and ran over to him.

"They already picked, so I dropped some money down," he said. "Did you see any numbers in them bones? Oh. You just saw good luck, huh?" Bump spoke so fast that Pee Wee missed half the words he said.

Across from them, a man took the dice in his hand and made an exaggerated shake before throwing them. The dice seemed to fumble around the small circle before landing on seven. Everyone cheered, and Bump grabbed his share of the money.

"Alright, Pee Wee!" Bump threw his arm around her shoulders and gave her a loving squeeze.

The men in the room began yelling "Pass! Pass!" or "You got lucky! Crap! Crap!"

These men were from all over: Black men, white men, Creoles, Cajuns, and even a few Chinese. And then there was Sam, standing by himself in the corner.

After about a half hour of watching, Bump elbowed her.

"Pee Wee, whatchu think?" Bump jostled her a bit.

"What I think about what? I don't know what's goin' on!"

"Should I keep going, or not?"

Pee Wee looked to the man in the corner. For some reason, she felt comfortable taking his advice when he gave her a thumbs up. She showed Bump a thumbs up, and he yelled, "Pass!"

The man with the dice sidled up next to Pee Wee and opened his hand to present them. "Maybe the lady wants to kiss the dice first? Go on, lil mama. Give us some good luck."

She looked at the hand-carved dice in his palm and turned her nose up. "No thank you."

"The lady says no! Y'all, we gonna do this?" He made a sweeping motion with his arm and threw. One of the dice twirled around on its corner before falling.

Eleven.

They all jumped up and cheered, and Bump grabbed his share of the money.

Pee Wee looked to Sam again. He made the signal for one more roll.

"Bump, I think this should be your last roll." Pee Wee whispered.

"Last? I'm just getting warmed up! C'mon, kiss the dice, Pee Wee! You is my good-luck charm!"

"I will do no such thing! Them dice been rollin' on the floor and in that nasty man's hand!"

Once again, the dice-thrower made a flamboyant shake of the dice before throwing them at the ground. He called out, "Lucky seven!"

Bump clapped his hands and jumped in the air.

"You win your money back yet?" Pee Wee asked.

"Yeah! And then some! I should keep playin'. I feel good about this next one."

"Well, I don't. I think you should stop while you's ahead."

"Don't be foolish! I'm goin' all in and doublin' down!"

Pee Wee reached out and grabbed Bump's wrist, "Look, this part right here is where I tell you to stop and you stop. Take yo' money and go. I need for you to listen to me on this."

One man yelled, "New shooter!"

A white man took over the dice.

"You lose that money, and I will root you to death, Bump. You understand? Let this one go."

Bump stared down into Pee Wee's eyes, and whatever he saw there caused him to shrug his shoulders and pocket the money. "Whatever you say, Pee Wee. Let's go."

"Come on, you lucky bastards!" the white man slurred before he rolled.

The room was silent as the dice rolled to a stop on the floor.

Bump's jaw dropped. "Snake eyes," he whispered.

"Is that good or bad?" Pee Wee whispered back.

"Bad. Very bad. Thanks for stopping me, Pee Wee."

Upon exiting the brothel, they bumped into Tiny.

"You get lucky, Bump?" Tiny asked as they walked by without saying a word.

"Maybe yes, maybe no," Bump said coldly. Now that Pee Wee had helped him win, he was determined to honor his half of the deal, which meant no more hanging with Tiny.

A dark feeling swept over Pee Wee, and she gasped at what she saw: Tiny's eyes were black like obsidian and shone just as bright. A voice in her head whispered, *"That boy possessed."*

"Bump," she said. Pee Wee reached out to grab him, but he was already heading back to go with Tiny. "Bump!"

Worried now, she reached inside her pockets for something small, something she had carried with her because Lone Wolf told her she would need it tonight. After not finding it in her pockets, she knelt down and found it in the cuff of her pants.

With the item now in hand, she got between Bump and Tiny and stretched up as far as she could on her tip toes, where she pressed the shiny black rock against Tiny's forehead and shouted, "Spirit, be gone!"

She didn't feel the knife go into her side. She just pressed the stone harder and harder into Tiny's forehead and yelled over and over, "Spirit be gone! Spirit be gone!"

Finally, Tiny stumbled backward, away from her, and growled at her loudly. The sound echoed down the alley before he turned and ran back out to the street.

Bump stared at Pee Wee in horror. His face had gone pale.

"He had somethin' evil in him, Bump," Pee Wee explained. "Somethin' bad."

But Bump just kept staring, wide-eyed. His lips moved without a sound. He pointed to the knife wound in her side.

Pee Wee laughed a little until she felt the spot Bump was pointing at. It hurt. When she pulled her hand back, it was covered in blood.

"Bump?" she said.

Her knees knocked together, and she felt like she was falling. She struggled to stand, but then collapsed. For a moment, it felt like her pa had caught her.

"I got you," she heard, before everything went dark.

"**WHY WOULD TINY** do such a thing?"

Aunt Teddy sat on the edge of the bed, tending to Pee Wee's side.

"Cuz he was possessed. I saw it in his eyes. Somethin' was wrong with him, Aunt Teddy." Pee Wee's voice was tired and raspy.

Aunt Teddy helped the girl sit up.

"Am I gonna die?" Pee Wee asked.

"No. Lucky for you, it missed anythin' vital. I was able to stitch you up, but you gonna have a nasty little scar there now."

"How long I been out for?"

"A day or so."

"Where's Bump?"

"Said somethin' about a jawbone. You doin' rootwork without me?"

"Just tryin' to get stronger, Aunt Teddy. That's all."

Just then, Bump rushed into the room. He spoke in huge gasps because he was out of breath.

Aunt Teddy jumped up so that Bump could rest on the bed. "Breathe, Bump. What happened?"

"Tiny… Tiny is dead."

"What? What do you mean, he's dead?"

"They must've got him," Bump said.

"Who?"

"Some white boys we throw dice with. They wouldn't let him throw that night he stabbed Pee Wee, so he followed one of 'em home and robbed him. Next day, a bunch of men caught up to him and hung him from a tree."

Pee Wee got up from the bed and put a robe on over her pajamas. "Where he at now, Bump?"

"You don't wanna see him, Pee Wee. It ain't pretty. Spare yourself, I'm beggin' you." Bump hung his head in shame.

"Pee Wee's right," Aunt Teddy said. "We need to see him, and you gonna take us there."

BUMP LED TEDDY and Pee Wee through the woods and away from their land, over to the whiter side of the parish. They eased through the crowd of black bodies and brown bodies pressed together as some of them wailed at the sight.

Pee Wee looked up at what was left of Tiny. His charred body hung from a tree, a chain around his neck. His clothes were burned off, and his face was contorted in sheer agony. His hands had fused to the chain around his neck while hopelessly attempting to pull himself free. He'd been fighting throughout the entire process.

"Who would do such a thing?" Pee Wee said.

"He stole from a white man," said Bump. "Y'know we ain't s'posed to do nothin' like that."

Pee Wee looked to Aunt Teddy. "Can we bury him in our cemetery, at least?"

"His folks will come get him later, I'm sure. They'll bury him proper."

"At least let me pray for him." Pee Wee started to push her way through the crowd, but her aunt stopped her.

"No," Aunt Teddy told her. "His folks got they own traditions. The best thing you can do right now is to let them be." She grabbed Pee Wee by the shoulders and turned her so she could look into her face. "Promise me you won't ever do somethin' stupid like this. Promise."

"What? You mean steal from a white man? I don't understand, Aunt Teddy! That wasn't Tiny. He was possessed! Somethin' was in him! He would never—"

Bump covered Pee Wee's mouth with his hand. "Yes,'m," he said to Aunt Teddy. "We promise."

Bump then dragged Pee Wee down the path until no one could hear them.

"What's wrong with you, girl? You bein' a great conjure woman don't mean nothin' to white folks. In they eyes, you'll always be a nigger. Do you understand me?" He moved in real close to her. "I'll always be a nigger, and Aunt Teddy will, too. So don't go thinkin' your Hoodoo or Voodoo or whatever is gonna save us, cuz it won't. And there ain't nothin' you can do about that."

Pee Wee stared at Bump's face for a few minutes until she felt the tears burning her eyes and stinging her cheeks. "You listen to me, Bump. I ain't never gonna be nobody's nigger. You understand? I'm gonna be somebody. I'm gonna get outta this town and make those white folks respect me. They ain't never gonna touch me or mine the way they did Tiny."

Bump shook his head, "And how you gonna do that, huh? What? You think Hoodoo is gonna make you rich?"

"Made you rich last night."

"That was luck, Pee Wee. You were just throwin' stuff around and makin' guesses."

Pee Wee stepped back like his words had physically assaulted her. "Says you, Bump. You'll see."

"See what?"

"The back of my head, cuz I'm leavin' this place and ain't never comin' back. Just remember that whenever you hear the wind blow or see leaves shakin' on a tree, that's gonna be me, comin' back to tell you to kiss my ass."

Pee Wee pushed Bump and stomped down the path. She had no more time for his foolishness. She had work to do.

VIOLA'S HOUSE OF VOODOO AND HAUNTED SPIRITS

WHENEVER MA WOULD tell me the story of how I came into this world, she'd always talk about how cold it was and how she and Pa had to wait forever for the midwife to come birth me. The midwife liked to drink, see, and when she finally got to our place, she was so drunk she could barely remember why she was there. She had a bottle of liquor with her and even offered a drink to Ma. Ma was horrified, but Pa just snatched that bottle and took a big swig for himself before telling the midwife to move outta his way.

"I think you done enough, Maylene," he told the midwife. He then stood at the foot of Ma's bed and clapped his hands before holding them open, waitin' like he was gonna catch a ball or somethin'.

Ma kicked him hard cuz she said that I kicked her hard first—she used the word "retribution"—then she told everybody to get out, sayin' she would birth me "her damn self."

While Cousin Skeet splashed cold water on Maylene's face to sober the midwife up, Ma grabbed the bottle of liquor from Maylene and took a swig, wincing at the taste. She told Maylene to get ready, then gave one big push and there I was.

Maylene held me up for my ma to see. Ma said she could barely see anythin' cuz Maylene had pulled a sheet up over her belly, and Pa started cryin'.

"Lord…" Maylene said. "She's so small. Look at this lil girl, Loretta."

They cleaned me up and wrapped me in a blanket. Then Pa carried me around the room, sayin', "This here is my lil Pee Wee! Look at lil Pee Wee!"

Ma got mad and told him she needed to feed me. So Pa passed me back to her, and I drank from my ma right away. Ma and Pa said I was so greedy. But I don't blame myself. I needed that milk to get bigger and stronger so that I could make my mark on the world.

Cousin Skeet held me next and talked to me like I was grown and could understand her. "If'n yo' nickname is Pee Wee, it's a powerful thing. You strong and unpredictable. And with me around, ya got no choice but to be strong, lil girl."

"Hattie Mae." Ma said.

"Hattie Mae?" Pa asked.

"After my grandma. I wanna keep the name alive. Hattie Mae." Ma smiled and pointed at me.

Pa smiled at Ma and said, "Well, welcome to this world, Hattie Mae Conway."

And that is the story of my birth.

I'm thinking about that story again because today is my birthday—my fourteenth birthday, to be exact. I wanted to spend it alone—I didn't want to see nobody, or talk to no one, especially not Bump—but after Teddy gave me some stuff (warm boots and a new coat), Lone Wolf came over and gave me some *more* stuff (a whole buncha pralines and a yellow cake with chocolate icing—my second-favorite treat to pralines and car'mels). The reason I don't wanna see no one is because this mornin', I got a package in the mail from Ma. She sent me a card and some money. Inside the card was a letter that I must've read a million times while layin' in bed and cryin'. It made me so very sad. It read somethin' like this:

Hattie Mae,

I never thought the day would come that I'd miss hearin' you and your sisters rippin' and runnin' through the house, yellin' and fightin'. This new house is so quiet, and I'm sure the mice don't even like it. I'm not sure if y'know yet, but Ann moved out. She went up north to see Betty and her son. (Betty is married now—to a half-Injun man—and they have a tiny baby together. The baby has bright red hair, and they call him Al.) Ann say he's small like you were. I hope I get to see him soon.

As for Ann, she was so angry with everybody when we moved. She kept actin' out so much. She was always cursin' and yellin' and just so angry. Whenever I tried talkin' to her, she ran away from home. Sheriff up here got tired of lookin' for her, so I had to put her in the girls home. I really tried hard with her, but I guess bein' with the three of y'all held Ann together. When I went to visit her at the home, I told her to wait and that you was comin' soon, but after a year of us fussin' and fightin', she told me that she'd had it and was gonna go see the world on her own. The girls home called me soon after that and told me she ran away. Couldn't find her.

After she sent me a letter sayin' that she was up north with Betty, I didn't hear from her again for awhile. Recently, though, she sent another letter to tell me she was movin' west. Accordin' to her, the government is just givin' away free land out there, or so she heard.

I know you is only fourteen now, but maybe you should think about movin' out there with her. I fear she is lonely. 'Sides, I'm sure ain't no Hoodoo gals out west, so you'd be the only one. Either way, it's almost time for you to get married and learn a trade. Pa and I paid for you to go to the finishin' school, and they's waitin' for ya whenever you's ready. Pa would be real proud. Look at Betty. She was in the program and now she's workin' at fancy hotels. Last I heard, she and Al are movin' to Chicago for work. She has some friends there, I guess.

And you tell that swamp rat Aunt Teddy I says thanks again for watchin' you and good luck with her baby. I can't wait for you to come visit. It's real quiet here, and I know there's enough woods for ya to run off in, that you'll like it a lot. I don't quite know how to say this, but you're also gonna be a big sister soon. I think it's a boy, so you'll have to come up here and make sure he don't turn into somebody like Bump. That boy keep trouble on his tail. Here's a few dollars and a train ticket. Try to get up to Chicago to see yo' sister. Oh, and thank yo' Pa in heaven, will ya? I'm sure he's smilin' down on you like always.

I miss you, Hattie Mae.

Love,

Ma

After readin' the letter one last time, I packed it up and got my coat. "I'm goin' for a walk!" I hollered to Aunt Teddy on the way out. I didn't bother listenin' for a response.

The walk to my family's old house felt strange. The ground was cold and hard, and the world was silent. Yeah, I heard the frogs and stuff, but I never heard somebody runnin' home from school or see someone fishin'.

The only person I did see was a tall, thin man, with cocoa skin, dressed in a suit jacket and straw hat, standin' at the cemetery gates and lookin' about absently, like he was just waitin' for someone to arrive. When he saw me, he smiled and said, "Happy birthday, Pee Wee."

I stopped and looked at this fool. How did he know my name? And how did he know today is my birthday? Nobody besides my family knows my birthday. And I do mean *nobody*.

"How y'know who I am?" I asked.

In the cemetery behind him was a black dog, sniffin' at the graves.

The man stood up straight and adjusted his suit jacket. "You want a piece of candy, Pee Wee?" he asked. "I hear you like pralines." He held out a bag filled with the most delicious-smelling pralines I've ever smelled in my entire life. Smelled like the butter and the sugar had melted together just right. And the pecans, well they *had* to have been freshly harvested.

"Or would ya prefer beignets?" the man said. He wiped his hand in front of the bag like he was doin' some sort of magic trick on it, and immediately, I smelled beignets. When he removed his hand, the bag had been replaced by a plate of the freshest beignets I ever smelled, with a dish of warm chocolate sauce on the side.

I shook my head. Somethin' wasn't right. Nothin' could smell so heavenly. But when he lowered the plate in front of me, my eyes and stomach said yes. I pinched my leg to make myself move.

But before I could take a step, the dog in the cemetery jumped the fence and blocked my way. Tail waggin', he dropped low on his front paws and started barkin' at me like he wanted to play.

I held my hand out to him, and he sniffed it, then started lickin' it.

"What's his name?" I asked.

"Lazarus," the man said.

"Like from the Bible? Man who rose from the dead."

"Ain't you a smart one, Miss Pee Wee. Y'know, she told me you was special, but I didn't believe her. I mean, how could a thirteen-year-old—"

"Fourteen." My face felt hot, like I was blushin' somethin' awful

He laughed. "How could a fourteen-year-old girl like yourself bind a grown Voodoo woman like her? And bid her to be your slave, no less."

He was talkin' about Viola, I knew that much. But if he knew Viola, then… "Who are you?" This man was gettin' under my skin.

He took off his hat and bowed his head. "That's a complicated question, Miss Pee Wee. But you can call me Pete."

"What're you doin' outside this here cemetery, aside from botherin' me, Pete?"

Lazarus kept lickin' my hand, like I was tastier than a candied praline.

The man held his heart, pretendin' as if to be wounded by my words. "I ain't tryin' to bother you. I just wanted to wish you a happy birthday. That's all."

I looked at that man and his black dog for a long time before I excused myself and kept walkin'.

"Viola told me about you," the man shouted after me. "Told me how you bound her. I'm impressed. But I gotta know: how could you do somethin' so selfish? Huh? How could you do a thing like that right after we was all just set free?"

I stopped and turned back to the man. The plate of beignets was gone now, replaced by a pipe and matches. He put the pipe to his mouth and lit it. The tobacco he used smelled like sweet cherries, and the pleasant scent lifted my nose.

"I don't know nothin' about no bindin'. No Viola, either," I said. "And we don't talk about slavery down in these parts."

I turned and started walkin' again. After I'd put some distance between us, I heard him yell after me once more, "You can't lie to me, Pee Wee! You're gonna have to face the truth sooner or later!" Then I heard him right in my ear, his voice swirlin' around me like that cherry tobacco smoke. *"I got whatchu want,"* he whispered. *"If'n you agree to help me, I'll give it to ya."*

I stopped walkin' and looked around, but there was no one there. His breath was on my neck now. *"I'll give you the one thing you need to be the most powerful conjure woman alive. That* is *whatchu want, isn't it?"*

The wind whispered all around me, and it was Viola's voice I heard next. *"Take the deal, Pee Wee. Let him help you like he helped me."*

"Help you?" I shouted. "Don't make me laugh! He can't help you! You mine! And you gonna be mine forever!"

"Let him teach you. He's waitin' for you at my place."

"How is you callin' me Viola? How you talkin' when you been bound?"

"That's one of his specialties. He's a Voodoo man, Pee Wee. He controls the will of the dead. And if y'know what's good

for ya, you'll come to my house and meet with him before he throw a spell on you."

I stomped my foot on the ground and cracked my knuckles "real unladylike," as Pa used to say. As if this day couldn't get any worse. There was only way to get to the bottom of all this. "Fine," I said. "I'm on my way."

As I walked through my old town on the way to Viola's house, I heard the voice of Cousin Skeet calling to me from the porch of my family's old home. When I looked her way, she laughed and opened her arms wide. "Don't think I forgot what day it is!" she said. "Bring it in for old Skeet!" She wiggled her outstretched fingers like a baby who wants somethin' from an adult.

Only thing is, Cousin Skeet ain't never moved her fingers like that before. And that's when I noticed the ground: it had turned cold and hard again.

"Bump is at work," Cousin Skeet continued. "But I got some stew brewin' inside if'n ya wanna join me. I cooked it up special for ya."

Before I could answer, a man stepped outta the house and onto the front porch with Cousin Skeet. It was him again. Pete.

I shook my finger and pointed at him, all accusatory-like. "What's he doin' here?" I said to Cousin Skeet.

Cousin Skeet looked around, all puzzled. It was like she couldn't see the tall man in the straw hat just standin' right there behind her.

"You ain't welcome here!" I hissed at him. "Go on now! Git! I'll meet ya where I told you I'd meet ya!"

Cousin Skeet looked around again to see no one. She looked back at me, all angry now. "Girl, what are you on about? Have you lost your mind? Just cuz it's yo' birthday, don't mean you can have a laugh at ol' Skeet. Now stop foolin' and come have some supper." On her way back into the house, she shuffled past Pete like she didn't even see him. As the door closed behind her, he stared at me for a moment 'fore followin' her inside.

I sprinted up the front steps and into the house after them. When I opened the door, I was hit with the most mouthwaterin' smells: biscuits drowned in butter and honey; every vegetable from the garden boiling in a pot on the stove; a bouquet of flowers on the kitchen table, set between two plates, one for me and one for Cousin Skeet.

The sight left me speechless. It almost felt like home. *Almost.* "Skeet…"

As if readin' my mind, Cousin Skeet waved away my gratitude. "Y'know you's like my own blood," she said. "I couldn't let number fourteen go by without doin' somethin' special for ya. C'mon, this is Cousin Skeet we're talkin' about!" She clapped her old arthritic hands together and cackled.

That's when the voice of Pete whispered in my ear. *"Like whatchu see? This here is my work. This is the kind of power I can promise you."*

When I looked around again, Cousin Skeet was gone. Nothin' was cookin' on the stove, and the cabin smelled like damp wood and ash. I turned to see Pete standin' at the door, smilin'. He laughed as he took a swig from a brown bottle he was now holdin'.

"Get outta my house, devil," I told him. "I ain't invite you in."

Pete laughed again. "I ain't see no salt line," he said, pointin' to the dark wood floor.

"I ain't need no salt line to bless this house," I said.

The grin on his face disappeared. He snapped his fingers and there we were, standin' outside my house.

"Don't you want these powers, Pee Wee?" he said. "Don't you wanna be feared like me?"

I looked down the road to Viola's house. *Maybe if I burned the house down—*

"You'd get rid of her, but not me," the man said.

He was in my head! Readin' my thoughts! *I'll give him somethin' to read!*

The man smiled devilishly. "A Bible verse? Really?"

I marched up the road to Viola's house. "Book of Thessalonians. 'In flamin' fire, inflictin' vengeance on those who do not know God and on those who do not obey the gospel of our Lord Jesus.'"

"No need to quote the scriptures for me, Miss Pee Wee. What? You think I don't know God? Or Jesus? I know Him better than you."

I walked the rest of the way in silence. Once inside Viola's house, I pulled the binding from my pocket and called out to her. "Show me where you at, woman!"

I saw a shadow move in the corner of my eye, and turnin' in that direction, I saw Viola standin' by the door in a white dress and head wrap. She was still bound to the house, at least. I could see it in her face.

I turned back to Pete, who was still standin' outside the doorway, and said, "Underneath that floor and cross that doorway is some black salt. You ain't comin' inside." I pulled a stone from my conjure bag. "And I got this here onyx that I'm gonna put on her." I pointed back to Viola. "She ain't goin' nowhere either."

"Why you actin' like this?" Viola said to me. "Ain't I helped you?"

I pointed at Pete. "Who is this mean? And why'd you send him after me?"

"I'll tell you who I am," Pete said. And without any trouble at all, he stepped over the line of salt that guarded the doorway from beneath the floorboards and flicked his wrist, which made me drop the small onyx I held in my hand the same way I would've had someone slapped it from me. "Leave us, Viola," he said, lookin' right at her. "You done enough."

"Unbind me so I can cross over," Viola begged.

I took offense to this. She shoulda been beggin' *me* to unbind her, not him.

"Yeah," I said to Pete. "Unbind her. If'n ya can." I put my hands on my hips, defiant, feelin' like my conjure spell was stronger than anythin'. I was a fire, he was a tiny spark. But that's when he said somethin' I didn't expect.

"The girl still needs your help. Help her one last time, and in exchange, I'll let you pass."

Viola dropped to her knees and thanked him in what I think was a dozen different languages 'fore I lost count. "I'll make you a new veve, Papa! I'll get all the children and the liquor! Merci, Papa!"

Papa?

She looked at me and held up a finger. "One more time." And then she disappeared.

A bark came from outside, followed by Lazarus appearin' at the door. The dog strolled inside the house and laid down beside Pete.

Pete cleared his throat and removed the straw hat from his head. His hair was white, and his face looked so much older than I had realized. "Now to formally introduce myself," he said. "Papa Legba, at your service." He bowed.

Viola tried teachin' me about all the Voodoo gods once, but there were too many for me to remember, and tryin' to do so made my head hurt, so she never got very far. But I remember the legend of Papa Legba.

"I'm the one you meet at the crossroads," he told me. "You see me when you die. I'm the one who grants you passage into the afterlife." He smiled a big toothy smile, then cupped his hand and blew a cloud of dust my way, "This is what happens when you die, Pee Wee."

At the first sniff of the dust, my eyes grew heavy and my head slumped to the side like I was about to fall asleep right there on my feet. I took a step back so as to balance myself. "You ain't gonna kill me, Papa."

"I'm not tryin' to kill ya, Miss Pee Wee. I'm tryin' to show ya." He rolled his fingers like he was beckoning me toward him.

That's when I saw it.

I was runnin'. Runnin' hard through them woods like it was the last day of school, leaves and branches slappin' my bare skin. But there was also these things snakin' on the ground, tryin' to grab my legs. At the sight of 'em, I ran faster—faster than I ever have before. I ran until my heart started burnin' and my body started sweatin' somethin' fierce. Ran like I did from them white men outside Luton. Ran until I was in the middle of nowhere. Just a dirt road in front of me and behind me. And another dirt road to my right and left.

The crossroads.

The sun wasn't high in the sky, but it wasn't low neither. Everything looked hazy and orange. The air smelled like nothin'. Just air. I bent over and put my hands on my knees to catch my breath. I wanted to keep runnin', but I didn't know which way to go.

Papa Legba and Lazarus appeared in front of me. "When you get to this part, I tell you which way to go. If'n you go that way, well, you just keep runnin'. Your ma is that way, your pa is that way, and your sisters are over there."

He kept pointin' in different directions until I was so mad, I stomped my foot and closed my eyes. Concentratin' real hard, I started sayin' the tenth Psalm, "Why, Lord do you stand far off… In his pride the wicked man does not seek him; in all his thoughts there is no room for God. His mouth is full of lies and threats; trouble and evil are under his tongue—"

Papa laughed at me. "I ain't evil, Pee Wee. Try again."

"Yes you is! It's evil to do this to a child of God."

He laughed again. Even Lazarus seemed to smile while pantin' with his tongue hangin' out. "You are no child of God," Papa said.

"Am too! I was baptized by my pa when I was younger! In the river with the preacher man!

It felt like somethin' was unfulin' inside me. I kept sayin' the Psalm and was tryin' to think of another one when I remembered somethin'. Remembered my trip back to Luton after all the folks there disappeared. What I never told no one is that I found that Irish witch again. I found her, and she was happy to see me. So happy, in fact, that she wanted to give me a gift. She taught me somethin' that would always protect me whenever I was feelin' scared or troubled.

Out there on them crossroads, I did what she told me, and I didn't feel scared no more cuz I was bein' filled with light of the Holy Spirit. I raised my arms above my head to welcome the warmth of the Lord. He was runnin' through me, and it tickled. All the hairs on my body stood on end cuz He was in me, and I felt my feet lift off the ground.

Papa stopped laughin'. "What's this now?"

I thought about the witch and the life she pulled from nature. Thought about how everythin' around her died as she did so. How that life lifted her from the ground and into the air.

I pulled the same life as she did as I pointed down at Papa from my place in the sky. "I am filled with power and light. The goddess and my sisters will fight by my side. Lightning, come down and take this man from my sight."

I felt somethin' shoot down my arm like it was the barrel of a divine rifle and expel itself from my fingertips like a lightning bolt. It hit Papa right in the chest and knocked him off his feet.

A calmness swept over me as I felt a new ball of lightning swell in my stomach, then course into the tips of my fingers. My ancestors were with me, fillin' me with their spirit and their love. The Irish witch was with me too, fillin' me with her power and chantin' beside me as I raised my hands again.

Papa raised his hands up to stop me, but it was too late.

I pushed hard and shot another bolt of lightning into him. But this time, somethin' inside me snapped, and a darkness swept over my soul. A darkness that pulled me toward it and promised me more power than I could ever imagine. But I was no longer in the mood for tricks, so grinnin' like a cat that just caught herself a sneaky little mouse, I aimed once again at Papa and was about to strike him again with my divine powers, when I heard a voice in my head shout, "*STOP!*"

I closed my eyes and opened them again to find myself back in Viola's house. I sat on the floor and there, across from me, was a scorched spot on the floor where Papa once stood.

"*Well, well, well…*" his voice said. "*You almost got me.*" I turned to find him, but there was no one there.

"I told all y'all, I'm gonna be the strongest and the most powerful."

"*But not the most famous. Someone will come after you, and they will be remembered more.*"

Papa appeared in the house's doorway, and with a snap of his fingers, set the house on fire. Flames blazed all around me.

"As long as I'm known," I said to him. "I don't care who come after or who came before. I protect me and mine, not you and yours."

"You gonna need me, Pee Wee. I know it. And when that time comes, you *will* call me and I *will* come help, cuz I like you. Maybe one day I'll even convince you to marry me."

He was actin' tough, but when I looked into his eyes, I knew he was scared.

"When you need me, Pee Wee, you call me with these words: 'open the gate for me, Papa Legba, open the gate.' And when I return, I will thank you and the Loa." He paused. "To be honest with you, I thought today was gonna be your last, but I can see now that your work ain't done. I'll be back for ya, though."

And with that, he grabbed a cane from the air and walked into the flames.

Back outside, I watched Viola's house burn. Watched as different potions exploded inside that house like fireworks, expellin' all sorts of colored smoke into the air. The wind carried on it the bitter scent of burnin' patchouli and jasmine, and the awful stench of death. I watched a whole host of spirits rise up from Viola's burnin' house and disappear into the sky.

I raised my hand high into the air, then slammed it down like I was smashin' somethin', and the house shook. I repeated the motion with both hands this time, and the house made a loud crackin' sound 'fore crumblin' to the ground.

I laughed at the sight. "Everybody should fear Pee Wee," I said.

"Pee Wee!" someone called. I knew right away that it was the voice of Cousin Skeet, the *real* Cousin Skeet, comin' down the path to investigate all the commotion. I knew it was her cuz there ain't no mistakin' the way she always be cursin' under her breath.

I ran to her and gave her a hug.

Even from afar, her eyes were alight from the blaze.

"Devil finally came back for the old Voodoo place, huh," she said. Then she handed me a basket. A red cloth covered the top so as to hide what was inside.

"What's this?"

"Honey, hoecakes and some stew. Teddy said you was out walkin' around, so I come to find ya. Figure'd you'd head home, since I know how much ya miss your folks."

"You's my folks now, Skeet."

She chuckled, then coughed, then chuckled again.

I helped her inside my family's house, and we ate the stew, which tasted as good as it smelled. Fresh vegetables, some real nice cuts of beef. It filled my stomach and my soul.

"Happy birthday, Hattie Mae," Cousin Skeet said. She pulled a small package from the bottom of the basket and handed it to me.

"What's this?" The package was wrapped in paper and string.

"Open it."

My hands shook when I saw what was inside. It was a letter. A letter from my sister Ann.

Cousin Skeet smiled. "Just got it today. They was holdin' it for you at the post office."

I couldn't believe what I was seein'. In the upper right-hand corner of the letter was the date and the words, "Montana Homestead."

Today is my fourteenth birthday.

Betty is in Chicago.

Ann is in Montana.

And according to Ann's letter, she desperately needs my help. The letter reads:

> *Bring all the Hoodoo you got, little sister. I need it. This man is goin' to kill me.*

ACKNOWLEDGMENTS

Thanks so much!

I WOULD SINCERELY like to thank Scott Johnson and Paul "The Goat" Allen for dealing with my once a semester meltdown(s). You both were warned! I also want to thank "The Goat" and Jason L. for reminding me of who I am because I say it when I'm in doubt.

Thanks to Seton Hill University Popular Fiction Graduate Program and all the awesome folks I met there. (I'm still awe-struck to meet authors, so sorry Gwendolyn if I have a million pictures of us together.) It was a rough program, but I survived it! Thanks to Luca Franco for latching on and not letting go and being a great guy. I never felt alone on campus because you were there, but you will never, ever pick out hotels for us again.

Thanks Sadie Hartmann and Rob Carroll for taking a chance on me and taking all of my phone calls and emails. I know I can be annoying, but I am such a stickler for a schedule and making a daily list of what to get done.

Huge thanks to my bosses—Lunden and Melinda—for working with me on getting the time to work on my Master's. And Lunden for keeping me focused on it with her gentle pushes when I needed it.

Thanks to my sister Teri for reading the iterations of this book and being the de facto family historian—finding that info that I never knew existed. Thanks to AhXul Fuentes, friend and beta reader, and all my old critique partners. Thanks Dad for listening to me read parts out loud, and thanks Mom for adding some input here and there.

Thank you Sofia, my sweet girl, for asking if I'm okay when I sit with my laptop and write for several hours. You're the best kid and the best baker I know—aside from me, Mommy.

Thanks to all the podcasters for getting the word out and having a bunch of laughs (looking at you, *Genre Junkies*). Thanks to the Instagram followers that had no problem reaching out and telling me what they wanted to see in the second book. And they were not shy about it at all! I read every post, comment, and question.

Last, thanks to you, reader, for purchasing this book and continuing to read about the legacy I am leaving behind for everyone to discover.

—Tracy Cross

ABOUT THE AUTHOR

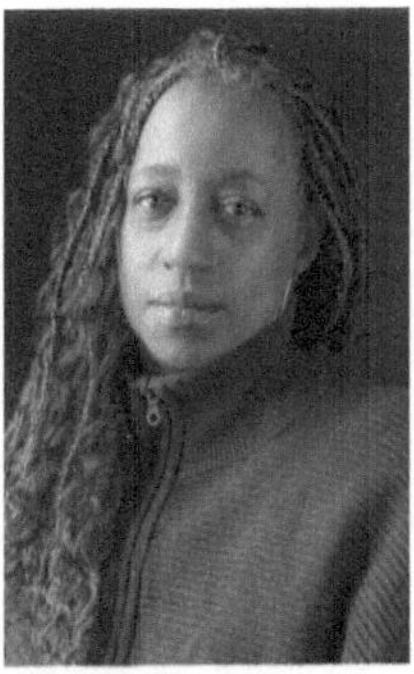

PHOTO © MIG DOOLEY

TRACY CROSS IS a celebrated African American author of horror, literary fiction, historical fiction, and magical realism. Her work explores themes of racism, sexism, karmic justice, and the power of family and faith. She enjoys disco and is a huge Prince fan. She lives and works in Washington, D.C.

For more information about Tracy's writing, visit her website at tracycwritesonline.com, or follow her via social media on Instagram @tracycrosswrites and X (formerly Twitter) @tracycwrites.

Monster Lairs: A Dark Fantasy Horror Anthology
Edited by Anna Madden
ISBN 978-1-958598-08-5

Frost Bite by Angela Sylvaine
ISBN 978-1-958598-03-0

Free Burn by Drew Huff
ISBN 978-1-958598-26-9

The House at the End of Lacelean Street
by Catherine McCarthy
ISBN 978-1-958598-23-8

When the Gods Are Away by Robert E. Harpold
ISBN 978-1-958598-47-4

The Dead Spot: Stories of Lost Girls
by Angela Sylvaine
ISBN 978-1-958598-27-6

Voracious by Belicia Rhea
ISBN 978-1-958598-25-2

Grim Root by Bonnie Jo Stufflebeam
ISBN 978-1-958598-36-8

The Bleed by Stephen S. Schreffler
ISBN 978-1-958598-11-5

Chopping Spree by Angela Sylvaine
ISBN 978-1-958598-31-3

Saturday Fright at the Movies
by Amanda Cecelia Lang
ISBN 978-1-958598-75-7

The Off-Season: An Anthology of Coastal New Weird
Edited by Marissa van Uden
ISBN 978-1-958598-24-5

The Threshing Floor by Steph Nelson
ISBN 978-1-958598-49-8

Club Contango by Eliane Boey
ISBN 978-1-958598-57-3

The Divine Flesh by Drew Huff
ISBN 978-1-958598-59-7

Psychopomp by Maria Dong
ISBN 978-1-958598-52-8

Disgraced Return of the Kap's Needle
by Renan Bernardo
ISBN 978-1-958598-74-0

*Haunted Reels 2: More Stories from the Minds of Professional
Filmmakers* Curated by David Lawson
ISBN 978-1-958598-53-5

Dark Circuitry by Kirk Bueckert
ISBN 978-1-958598-48-1

Soul Couriers by Caleb Stephens
ISBN 978-1-958598-76-4

Abducted by Patrick Barb
ISBN 978-1-958598-37-5

Cyanide Constellations and Other Stories
by Sara Tantlinger
ISBN 978-1-958598-81-8

Little Red Flags: Stories of Cults, Cons, and Control
Edited by Noelle W. Ihli & Steph Nelson
ISBN 978-1-958598-54-2

Frost Bite 2 by Angela Sylvaine
ISBN 978-1-958598-55-9

The Starship, from a Distance by Robert E. Harpold
ISBN 978-1-958598-82-5

Dark Matter Presents: Fear City
ISBN 978-1-958598-90-0